CENTRALIA: EPICENTER

CENTRALIA

There's a town in Columbia County, Pennsylvania that's been burning since 1962. Its name is Centralia and it's been ablaze for nearly sixty years. Why is no one talking about it? Because the Dark doesn't want us to. It wants to remain anonymous as it builds its army and strength beneath earth's surface.

The Dark has had a hold on Centralia since October 17th, 1868 when the borough's founder was murdered (sacrificed?) by members of the Molly Maguires, an Irish secret society. His three killers were later hanged on March 25th, 1878. Dead men tell no tales. In 1869 Father Daniel Ignatius McDermott cursed the borough, stating that the St. Ignatius Roman Catholic Church would eventually be the last building standing. Little did he know the curse would grant immense strength to the Dark.

Centralia, Pennsylvania wasn't the only epicenter for the Dark's power. It's evil strength spiked on March 25th, 1947 beneath the town of Centralia, Illinois, leading to a mine explosion that killed (sacrificed?) 111 people. 142 men had been trapped in the mine at the time. 65 were killed by the burns, 46 died later.

In May of 1962 the Dark's power leveled up yet again, igniting the mines beneath Centralia. Since then, it's slowly made the small town less and less inhabitable, driving away its citizens in order to keep its secrets. But its power had grown too immense to contain beneath these two Centralia towns. It stretched out to other Centralias across the United States, and quite possibly the world.

The following are the first in a series of ongoing tales about how six heroes found themselves in different Centralia towns, and how they faced down denizens of the Dark. Each of the towns have their own evil history, and the Dark's soldiers feed off of those sins making them formidable adversaries. Will our heroes survive their conflicts? Can they prevent the Dark from gaining more power? What happens when the Dark reaches full strength? Are you brave enough to stand with these brave heroes?

The answers start here...

Centralia: Epicenter

Grandma's Eyes 8
Heath Amodio; Centralia, WA

Sundown 48
Michael Patrick Hicks; Centralia, KS

A Certain Kind of Forest Sound 76
Adam Cesare; Centralia, TX

The Valley of the Yunwi Tsunsdi 92
Brian Keene; Centralia, WV

G.W. Bolt and the Case of the Grabbed Ghost 120
Brian Quinn; Centralia, NY

The Grasp of Wraiths 138
Cullen Bunn; Centralia, MO

Cover Art by Kealan Patrick Burke

Edited by Cullen Bunn and Heath Amodio

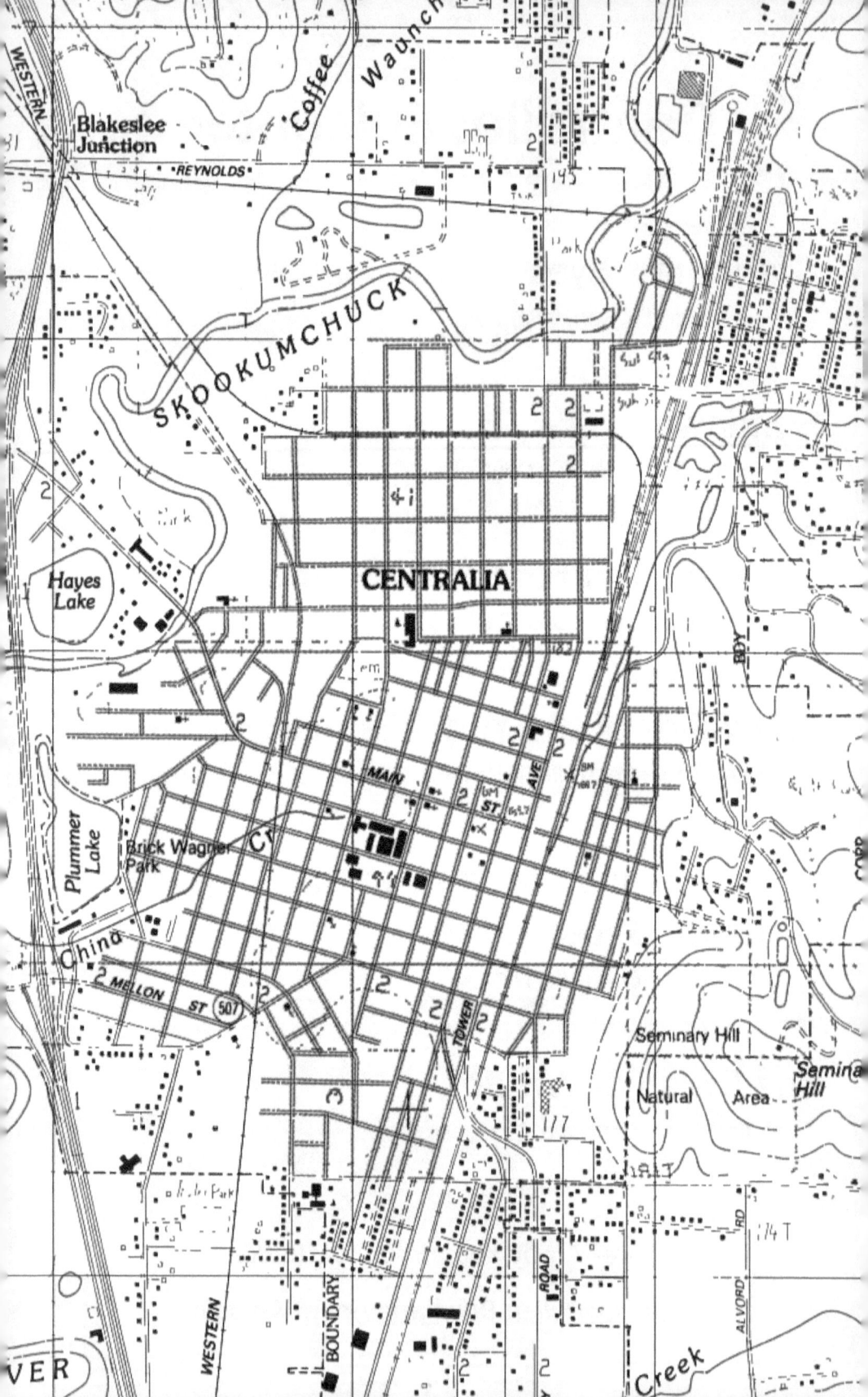

Grandma's Eyes

Heath Amodio

Centralia, WA

Location of Centralia, Washington

Coordinates: 46°43′14″N 122°57′41″W

Country	United States
State	Washington
County	Lewis

Area
- Total   7.81 sq mi (20.22 km2)
- Land   7.62 sq mi (19.74 km2)
- Water   0.19 sq mi (0.48 km2)

Elevation   187 ft (57 m)

Population
- Total   16,336

First Epicenter Sighting
- January 1994

Percent Burn
- 12%

People always told Jenna that she had her grandmother's eyes. If only they knew just how right they were. At that moment, as Jenna pretended to look out the passenger side window of her mother's 2002 Toyota Corolla, she just wanted eyes that worked. She imagined the endless rows of trees that lined the highway, and thought…

Why the fuck is Washington State so wet?

According to a quick Siri search, it rained an average of 213 days each year in Long Beach, and 210 days a year in Fork. Fork? Wasn't that where that book about the shiny vampires was based? God, that shit was miserable.

She'd fallen asleep during the first movie. Her friends left her there and an usher had to wake her up before they locked her inside. Her friends were dicks. She fucking missed them. It was the last time she'd gone to the theater before the car accident that stole her sight. What a shitty final movie.

It'd rained ever since they crossed the border from Oregon into Washington. Four hours of rain was more than she'd experienced in the last four months back home in Los Angeles. She was depressed by hour two. Not that she could see the gray skies or the rain splashing across the windshield. She didn't need to. The perpetual sound of the windshield wipers squeaking across the glass started to drive her crazy right away, and she could feel the weather in her bones, damp and cold.

How'd Grandma Marie deal with such a morose climate? No wonder the grunge movement started in such a dreadful state. It was the weather. It totally made sense that Washington was also the location of Silicon Valley. Everyone was cooped up inside 200 plus days a year. What the hell else was there to do but fiddle around with motherboards and… mouses? Was the plural still mice if it's not pertaining to the animal? What the hell kind of sad ass level of inner dialogue had she resorted to?

Shit, she was bored. She couldn't even use her earbuds because her mother wanted to "talk." All that meant was they'd hold brief, three-minute long conversations to fill the gaps between classic rock songs on the radio. Her mother would literally cut herself off mid-sentence if a Pat Benatar or Stevie Nicks song came on. Any excuse not to actually speak to her. Jenna was fine with that. She prayed for a Heart marathon that would keep her mother quiet for a good hour, dancing along to "Barracuda" or "Crazy on You." Jenna was more upset about being dragged to Centralia, Washington, where the highest total of clear sunny days in a month was July, with a whopping 10. It wasn't like she could see the blue sky anymore, but she still enjoyed the sun on her face. The sun was a stranger to Washington. Just one more reason it was going to be a rough time at Grandma's.

She'd managed to avoid visiting her grandmother for the last five years. Last time they saw each other, Jenna was struck down with migraines so painful they made her throw up. It was weird. She couldn't be in the same room with her grandmother without a searing pain right between her eyes. As soon as the door closed between them, the pain would subside. Needless to say, they hadn't seen each other since.

There was no getting around seeing her now. Her mother didn't confide any actual information beyond the fact that her grandmother was "not doing well." It didn't take a genius to figure out just how *not well* she was. Jenna's mother wasn't emotionally available, but she wouldn't force migraine headaches on her daughter just to torture her either. She could be a dick, but she wasn't an asshole. No, if they were going to stay with her grandmother in Centralia, it meant Grandma didn't have much time left.

The thought of her grandmother's death only added to her depression. She'd heard countless stories about how amazing her grandmother was from her aunts and uncles. People too lazy to care for her in the end apparently. Hell, even her mother had bragged about Grandma a few times when the liquor was flowing. Yet, Jenna knew next to nothing about who her grandmother actually was.

Before the headaches, she'd been too young to care. There were too many toys to play with, games to play outside with the neighborhood kids. The headaches had started by the time she reached the age where she was curious about the older woman that sang Joni Mitchell or Carole King while she danced and baked in the kitchen. Now she'd never get to know her grandmother. Not unless she was willing to push through the pain and nausea, but was she? Could she?

Creedence Clearwater Revival's "Fortunate Son" ended, and the D.J. came on to preface the commercials. Jenna took a deep breath and prepared for her mother's three minutes of ad supported parenting.

"You okay, pumpkin?"

Jenna hated when her mother called her things like that. She was sixteen for crying out loud. Her mother had her young, eighteen, and all of her parenting came from 80's sitcoms. The kind where parents were SUPER engaged and every problem was solved within a half hour. Pumpkin, sweetie, peanut, sissy — that one was fucking weird — sugar, honey… the list went on. Sometimes, Jenna thought that her mother may have actually forgotten her name. Like that one simple-minded but kind looking President before

Obama, calling important people buckaroo because he clearly had no idea what their actual names were. What the hell was his name? It didn't matter. The nicknames were supposed to be endearing, but when her mother said them, they just sounded fake. It only got worse after the accident.

"Honey? You okay? Do you need me to find a rest-room or anything? Maybe some food? It shouldn't be too much longer, but we can stop."

"No. I'm fine."

"Are you cold? This damn rain. I can turn the heat on if you feel… I don't know. Damp or whatever?"

"Damp?"

"You know what I mean."

"Like moist?"

"Stop it. You know I can't stand that word."

"What word, moist?"

"Stop it. I mean it."

Jenna laughed. Sometimes fucking with her mother was the only thing that got her through the day. Even though she DID feel damp AND cold.

"Can you turn the heat on a little actually?"

"Of course, sweetheart."

Two commercials down. Only three or four more before another classic hit, and commercial break parenting would be placed on standby.

"I'm sorry about this. Taking you away from your friends during the summer. I feel awful."

"It's fine. Please stop apologizing. I can't deal."

Two more commercials down.

"I know you're dreading the headaches but I really think those prescription pills the doctor gave us will help."

"I didn't know they made pills just so you can be around your own grandmother. Seems really specific."

"You don't HAVE to be a wiseass all of the time, you know? Sometimes it'd be nice if-

Janis Joplin's raspy folksy blues vocals started to play, and Jenna's mother turned up the volume.

"Oh my God, I love this song."

It was one of Jenna's least favorite tracks. She didn't understand the point of a song all about Janis begging for a Mercedes Benz, but they were different times, she supposed. At least the discussion was over. She'd have ten to fifteen minutes of silence from her mother.

The squeak of the windshield wipers cut off.

"Well, that's convenient. We just passed the sign for Centralia and the rain's stopped. I guess we were closer than I thought. Roll down your window, sweetie. We're almost there."

Jenna did and the intoxicating clean scent from the just finished rainstorm, blended with the minty aroma of endless pine trees, made her breathe deep. She pictured the endless green forest stretched out on all sides and wished she could see it. Her friend Tammy told her it was the most green she'd ever seen in her life when her family drove through Washington last summer. All Jenna could do was imagine the last time she'd seen a forest, copy and paste the image over and over again.

It didn't do the trick.

Then she heard the whispers for the first time. Hushed voices speaking so softly that she couldn't make out what they were saying, but so many of them it felt as if they were screaming. She had no idea how she could hear them over the car's radio. Her hearing had definitely gotten sharper since losing her eyesight, but still.

"Do you hear that?"

"What?"

"Can you turn the radio down?"

"But it's John Fogerty. "Centerfield," sweetie. Classic."

"Please, Mom."

The whispers, if she could even call them that, intensified. They came from all around her. A roar of soft voices.

Her mother finally clicked off the radio and the car was filled with the whispers.

"That, the voices, do you hear the whispers?"

"I-I don't hear anything, pumpkin. What's it sound like?"

"Like a crowd of people talking to each other. Real low but there's so many. It's like white noise."

Jenna could picture the look of concern that was surely spread across her mother's face. It was undeniable in her voice.

"Um, can you hear what they're saying?"

"They're all talking over each other. I think they're only saying one word but I can't be sure."

"What's the word?"

"Leave."

***

The whispers persisted right up until they turned onto her grandmother's road. Rolling the windows up didn't even help. Her mother blasted the car's radio, but the whispers still rang through. There was no doubt about it. Whoever or whatever was talking in the woods, definitely DID NOT want them there. Jenna was ready to scream as they turned onto her grandmother's road, but the whispers cut off at once, as if someone had simply clicked off a radio.

"Are you okay?"

"Yeah. They've stopped. What was that, Mom?"

"I wish I knew. I didn't hear anything. At least whatever it was seems to be over now."

Yeah, thought Jenna. *Now I'll just have the searing pain in my head to worry about. Big step up.*

She knew her mother was beyond freaked, and maybe being around Grandma would calm her down. Part of her wished she could have that same option, but Grandma brought her the opposite of peace.

Her mother turned off the car and they climbed out. Jenna stood by the passenger door and aimed her head towards where she assumed the house would be. Dread threatened to overwhelm her. She felt like she'd rather deal with the whispers. It was crazy to feel that way. Of course it was. But the whispers only scared her. Grandma caused her real pain.

"We can unpack the car later, okay? I wanna check on your grandmother."

"I can start unpacking now."

Anything to keep from going inside yet.

Her mother stepped around the car and placed her hands on Jenna's shoulders.

"I know you want to be more independent, sweetie, but unloading the car is something we're gonna have to do together. I don't want you trying to carry bags up these stairs. What happens if your hands are full and you trip, and you can't break your fall?"

"I'm not an idiot, Mom. I'm blind. Not stupid. Obviously, I can't lug our bags into the house. I wouldn't even know which direction to walk. I can unload it from the car to the driveway though."

"I know what you're doing. You've been taking the prescription migraine pills for three days now. They've built up in your system, and they're going to help. I'm sure of it."

"You're always so sure of everything. How often does that actually work out for you?"

"Not as often as I'd like, but it's better than not hoping at all."

"Is that how you think I feel? Hopeless?"

"No! And I pray you never do. I'm just saying there's no harm in thinking positively."

"And if the pills don't work?"

"Then we'll cross that bridge if we have to. Let's go check on your grandmother. She's excited to see you again. It's been way too long."

Her mother took her hand and guided her up the stairs. Each step felt like she was walking towards a burning house. Any moment the flames would engulf her, making her scream with pain.

They reached the front door and her mother knocked. Jenna heard her mother turn the doorknob and open the door. It swung with a low dull creak.

"Hello? Mom?" said her mother. "It's Toni and Jenna."

"I'm in my new bedroom. Here in the back," said her grandmother from somewhere deep in the house.

"You ready, sweetie?

"I guess so."

"Okay. Here we go."

They entered the house. Jenna felt for the door and pushed it closed.

"Nicely done."

"Seriously? I didn't park the car. I closed the door, Mom."

"I know, but still…"

"Are you two coming or not?"

"On our way, Mom. Hold your horses."

Where would my mother be without the eighties and their phrases, thought Jenna. *Then again, that saying is probably from a time where horses were more prevalent. Good thing she didn't say the joke out loud. Her mother could've turned it on her. That would've been embarrassing.*

Jenna tried to lose herself in her own idiotic mental rantings, but it was no use. She kept hoping the pills would work. Please work. Please work. Please, please, please work. She took slow deliberate steps as her mother guided her further and further into the house. Her mother let out small frustrated breaths and clicked her tongue whenever Jenna let any tiny obstacle slow them down.

"I'd like to see your grandmother at some point today, pumpkin."

"I think I'm good here."

"Here? We're in the dining room."

"Then there should be plenty of chairs, right?"

"Yes, but her bedroom door's right there."

It must be closed, thought Jenna. Pills be damned, if the door was open, she'd be in pain. She was sure of it.

"Just turn a chair in my direction and I'll handle the rest."

"We need to know if the pills work, sweetie. We're going to be here for quite awhile."

"You hope," said Jenna before she could stop herself.

Her mother dropped her hand. She'd really hurt her. She felt like an asshole.

"Yes. I do," said her mother.

Jenna had to change the subject. She was starting to spiral for being such a bitch to her mother. Wasn't it bad enough her grandmother was dying, and she was the reason her mother hadn't spent more time with her? She wouldn't ruin whatever time they had together before her grandmother died. The weight of that guilt, it'd be too much.

"I think we'll know when you open the door," said Jenna with a false cheerfulness that made her ill.

"How'd you know her door was closed?"

"Took a guess. I had a 50/50 shot at being right."

"Fine. Sit here."

Her mother turned a chair and Jenna sat down on the hard wood of the seat. She heard her mother walk across the room. Jenna gripped the curved ends of the armrests on the dining room chair, digging her nails into the grooves of the chair's antique craftsmanship. Her mother opened the door.

Searing hot pain erupted between Jenna's eyes! She wanted to scream out. NO. Jenna refused to do that. Her mother needed this. She'd deal with the fucking pain.

"Fu-

Jenna bit down on the flesh between the thumb and forefinger on her right hand. The pain in her hand was sharp, instant, but it only dulled the headache for a few seconds. She fought back the urge to vomit as her stomach lurched. Tears rolled down her cheeks and she turned away from her grandmother's room. She couldn't let her mother see her crying.

Please close the door. The thought screamed out in Jenna's head. She dug her knuckles into her temples, praying for something to work, anything. The pain in her head shifted from between her eyes to her temples. Split in two, the agony wasn't as unbearable. Her stomach settled.

Her temples started to burn. She couldn't keep the pressure up for much longer. Her arms were tired. Her knuckles slipped, losing the pressure points on the sides of her head. The agony rushed back between her eyes with such sudden intensity that she couldn't fight back the bile anymore. She bent over as the muscles in her stomach tightened, giving her no choice but to throw up partially digested rest stop food.

"I'm sorry," she said as she pushed herself to her feet. She'd thrown up. The pain should've subsided. Yet it threatened to knock her to the floor.

Jenna had failed. It only took thirty seconds to ruin her mother's time with her grandmother. She had to get out of the house. She was embarrassed and mixing that with the pain was making her want to die.

"Jenna?"

Her mother called, but she couldn't answer. If she opened her mouth, she'd hurl again. She'd already made a mess. She wasn't gonna add to it.

Slamming into the dining room table, chairs, and walls, Jenna managed to make her way through a door and into another room. She touched something cold and metal. A kitchen appliance of some sort, she assumed.

"Jenna, sweetie, stop before you hurt yourself."

Didn't her mother understand? She was trying to get away from what was hurting her.

If she was in the kitchen, that'd mean the front hall was to her left. She turned left and her foot got caught on the corner of something. Jenna fell hard. She smacked down on the cool linoleum floor stomach first. If she'd had any kind of breasts to speak of she might not have nailed her chin on the floor too. Unfortunately, she was still an A-cup. Something she blamed on youth sports, gymnastics and cheerleading mostly. Her chin split and she bit her tongue. Reaching up to touch beneath her lips, Jenna felt something warm and wet. She smelled the iron of the blood that ran between her fingers.

Stupid, she thought.

"Jesus, Jenna!" said her mother as she dropped to her knees beside her. "What were you thinking?"

"What's going on out there?"

"Nothing, Mom. Jenna tripped and fell but she's okay."

That's debatable, thought Jenna.

Her mother rolled her over and helped her sit up. The pain in her tongue and chin had distracted her from her headache, but it came back with a vengeance.

"I can't take it," said Jenna. "My head hurts too much."

"Let's get you outside for a bit."

Jenna's mother helped her to her feet. She led her over to the counter, and Jenna placed her hand on the smooth top.

"Lean here for a second. I need to wet a cloth so I can clean that cut on your chin."

"I can't, Mom. I'm gonna be sick. You have to get me out of here."

"Honey-"

"PLEASE."

Her mother ducked under her right arm and wrapped one arm across Jenna's shoulders. She straightened up and took all of her daughter's weight onto herself.

"What's going on out there, goddammit?" asked her grandmother from somewhere behind Jenna. She'd never heard her grandmother curse before. It didn't sound right to her ear.

Stay in your room, Grandma, Jenna thought.

She was surprised by how easily her mother was able to turn them completely around. Jenna felt like she was dead weight, but her mother led them down the hallway towards the front door.

"We're almost there, sweetie."

"I'm sorry, Mom."

"Don't be ridiculous. This is my fault."

Jenna felt the breeze on her sweat-coated skin and smelled the pine trees as they stepped through the front door.

"We're at the steps. There are five."

Stepping out and down, Jenna thought about the time she took a nosedive down a dozen steps because they were an inch off from what she was used to. She'd spent three months with a cast on her wrist. Because of ONE FUCKING INCH.

These steps gave her no such problem. She stepped off the final stair and onto the soft grass of the front yard. The headache had subsided just enough to alleviate any desire to stab herself in the temple, but it still knocked her feet out from under her. She tumbled forward and her mother held on enough to slow her descent.

The grass was cold and wet. It felt good on her neck and back. Twenty minutes earlier she was complaining about those same conditions. Anything felt better than the ungodly pain she felt in the house.

"Toni?"

"Stay in the house, Mother."

"What's wrong with Jenna?"

"She's got another headache. Please stay inside. I'll be right in. I need to figure out what to do. Jenna can't stay here."

"Let me see her."

"No! Please, Mother. You can't be near her. I have no idea what the hell is going on between you two but it's obviously real."

That's when the whispers started again. They roared like a freight train crashing into Jenna's ears. She slammed her hands down on her ears, pinning them to her head so hard they hurt. The sheer agony of her own scream scared her. She wasn't aware she was capable of such a feral sound.

"Mother!"

"I haven't left the kitchen. It can't be because of me."

Toni knelt down beside her daughter. She took Jenna's head in her hands.

"Talk to me, sweetie. Tell me how to help you."

LEAVE. LEAVE. LEAVE. LEAVE....

"The whispers... I can't... so loud!"

"Whispers? Honey, I don't understand."

"Enough of this, Toni. I know what the girl needs."

"Mother wait. It's too much for her."

"I've had enough of this nonsense. You know damn well what's going on. Just because you turned your back on it, doesn't mean it isn't real."

"No. I won't let you drag her into your insanity."

"LOOK AT YOUR DAUGHTER. Don't you hear her screams? Because I do. I feel them all the way to my bones. I don't know what you've done to yourself to get rid of the Push, and frankly I don't care. Despite all you've done to eliminate it from your bloodline, it's strong in Jenna. Now move to the God damn side before I move you myself."

Jenna had no idea what her grandmother was talking about. She barely made out every other word between the army of whispers. Jenna closed her useless eyes tight as if it'd help. All she wanted to do was get the hell out of Centralia, Washington. She longed for LA where the sun sat high, there was more fire than rain, and she didn't have to deal with crippling pain.

Then there was an unfamiliar hand on her wrists. The fingers were thin and all knuckles. The skin was tight, smooth, and cold to the touch. They had to be her grandmother's hands. She realized it was the first time she'd ever felt them on her skin, and she was surprised they didn't burn her flesh.

There was a warmth where her grandmother held her, but it wasn't painful. It soothed her. The whispers slowly started to diminish, and her headache started to subside. There was an energy coursing through her. She'd never felt anything like it before. Her skin prickled against the wet grass. Every hair on her body stood up.

"Open your eyes, Jenna," said her grandmother.

Why? She thought. *What difference would that make?*

But Jenna listened. No matter how useless it seemed, it also felt... right. She slowly opened her eyes, starting with her right. Just a crack. Just enough to let the... light in? Excitement overruled caution and she opened both eyes wide. Bright light blinded her. She'd laugh about the irony of that later. Colors erupted into existence once again. Her mind associated each color with the objects she'd only seen in her memories for years. Green = grass and pine trees. Gray = the sky above Washington State. Brown = her mother's hair. Red = her own flushed cheeks.

"I... I can see."

"What, sweetie?"

"I can see... myself?"

"Because you're seeing through my eyes," said her grandmother.

But that was insanity. Like something out of a Richard Matheson novel. There's no such thing as magic or miracles. People don't suddenly see through someone else's eyes. Yet, that's exactly what she was doing according to her grandmother. There was no other explanation. Not a logical one anyway. Then again, logic had pretty much flown the coop.

Jesus, I sound like my mother, thought Jenna.

"Can you look at my mom, Grandma?"

Her grandmother turned and Jenna was able to look into her mother's eyes for the first time in years.

"Hi, Mom," she said.

"Oh my God," said Toni as she embraced her daughter.

Toni cried with a joyous smile spread across her face as Jenna's grandmother continued to grip her right wrist. Jenna's happiness quickly turned to fear as she looked through her grandmother's eyes into the trees that bordered her yard. There was something standing behind the trees. ALL of the trees. Their mouths moved and their whispers, less amplified, brushed past her ears. The hushed voices still gave their same warning, as the things glared at her with hate-filled eyes.

***

"Grandma, there's something in the woods."

"You see them already? Your power's even stronger than I thought."

"What's she talking about, Mother?"

"Look in the woods, Mom. Behind the trees," said Jenna.

Toni turned and looked into the trees, but shook her head in frustration.

"There's nothing there," she said.

"You can't see them because you gave up the right," said Jenna's grandmother.

"When will you stop blaming me for wanting a normal life? For not wanting people to think I'm crazy? Do you have any idea how hard it was growing up with every kid in school calling my mother the crazy witch lady?"

"Spare me your justifications. I've heard'em all a hundred times over. Most daughters would've told those kids to go fly a kite. Defended their mother. You never had any fight in you. It's good you gave up your gift. You wouldn't have lasted long."

"That's so sweet of you, Mother. Why-

"STOP FIGHTING!" Jenna yelled and thought at the same time.

Toni and her grandmother's knees buckled, and they were forced to lean on one another. Turning, they looked away from one another, and swallowed the rest of the fight.

"I can see. Isn't that all that should matter right now? How are we not celebrating this?"

"Because there's too much at stake to celebrate right now," said her grandmother.

"Here we go," said Toni.

"Mom. Stop. What do you mean, Grandma?"

"The things behind the trees, can you describe them for your mother, Jenna?"

Jenna stared at the things behind the trees but she couldn't find the words to describe them. She'd just regained her sight seconds ago. She wanted to enjoy the moment. There was so much beauty around her, but her grandmother wanted her to focus on the horrible things in the woods. It wasn't fair.

"Come now, child. We must convince your mother, or she'll never help us."

"Help us what?" Said Jenna.

"I'll explain everything in time. Tell her what you see. Now."

"Th-they look like people."

"Yes. Yes. But?"

"But some of them, men and women, their skin is dark gray. Like the color of ash. Their skin is cracked, like deep cuts in concrete."

"And their eyes, Jenna. What about their eyes?"

Why was her grandmother making her do this? She didn't want to take in the details of these wretched things. These dead people?

"Are they dead, Grandma?"

"Stop this, Mom. Can't you see you're scaring her?"

"She should be scared. We all should. Now, the eyes, girl. Describe the eyes."

"They're just… black holes. Endless. Like they go on past the back of their heads and into… nothingness."

"Good, and the others? The ones that aren't the color of ash?

"The others have blue skin, as if they were holding their breath for too long. And they're soaked. Completely drenched. Almost… waterlogged, I guess. They open their mouths like they wanna say something, but water pours out instead. There are men, and women, and — oh my God — children. Three of them."

"That's enough, Mom. I believe you, okay? Look away, Jenna."

Jenna turned to her grandmother, terrified. She couldn't stand to look at the dead people staring back at her anymore.

"What are they, Grandma? Zombies?"

"Don't be so foolish, child. They're Centralia's dead. They've come to warn us."

"Warn us about what, Mom?" said Toni.

"That God's going to try and wipe out this town again."

***

Jenna's grandmother dragged her through the house by her wrist. Her grip was painful. It reminded her of the time she played with her father's handcuffs. She'd wrapped one around her tiny wrist when she was eleven and closed it as far as she could. It'd clicked like machine gun fire as she clamped it closed and pinched her skin. She cried out and her father rushed down the stairs, grabbed the key from his policeman's jacket, and unlocked the cuff. Tears ran down her face as her father rubbed her wrist and spoke to her in his sweet voice, the one that was just above a whisper and made her feel invincible.

She'd give anything to hear his sweet voice now. He'd died one night while on the job. Her mother never told her what really happened. The casket was closed and she resented the fact she'd never have the chance to say a real goodbye. Toni told her it was better that way. Better to remember him the way he was. Like when he used the sweet voice.

They reached her grandmother's bedroom and finally stopped. Her grandmother relaxed her grip, and blood rushed into Jenna's fingers. She hadn't even noticed when they started to tingle. Looking around, she saw her grandmother's new bedroom for the first time. Books were everywhere. Overflowing bookcases lined every wall. More books were stacked on a desk at the end of her bed. All of them old hardcovers. A dozen stacks of ten or more. Still more books were stacked in a half circle around the bed. Jenna turned her head to look at the spines. It appeared each stack represented a letter in the alphabet. She counted the stacks and came up with twenty-four. One for each letter of the alphabet except for X and Z. There was even a tiny pile for Q.

She couldn't have possibly read all of them, she thought.

"Well I did. Most of them twice."

"You heard me? But, I said that in my head," said Jenna.

Her grandmother held up the wrist she was still grasping..

"How do you think you can see right now? We're connected, you and I."

"So you can hear everything I'm thinking?"

Even about my Dad?

"I'm trying very hard not to."

"Can I hear your thoughts?"

"Believe me, girl. You don't want to. You'll get everything I need to say all at once. I'm not sure you could handle that, and you damn sure wouldn't make any sense of it. I'm blocking my thoughts as best I can. You'll need to know what I'm thinking the second I think it, but not yet."

"Setting aside the fact that you've got some kind of intrusive mind-meld with my teenage daughter, and she can suddenly SEE, can we get back to the whole God's gonna wipe this town out thing?"

"I need that stack of books in the center of my desk."

Toni looked at her mother with an "okay, and" expression.

"If I let go of Jenna's wrist she won't be able to see what I have to show her."

Toni rolled her eyes, crossed the room to the desk, and lifted the high stack of hardcovers. They slammed against her chest.

"Jesus Christ, Mom. Ever hear of paperbacks?"

"They don't make THESE books in softcover."

"Of course not. Where do you want them?"

"Spread them out on the bed."

Jenna watched her mother struggle to the bed. She tipped the stack forward, and the heavy books toppled to the mattress.

"Careful. They're old."

"It's a bed, Mom. I think they'll be okay."

Toni spread the books out across the bed, nearly covering it from head to foot. Now that Jenna could see the tops of the old hardcovers, she noticed they had a ribbon holding a place in each one.

"Open them to the pages I have marked."

"Blurting out a please once in a while wouldn't kill you. Just saying," said Toni.

Toni did so. Once they were all opened, Jenna's grandmother started to explain.

"There have been TWENTY-SEVEN major floods in this town since 1887. They've killed fifteen people in all."

"Jonathan?" Asked Toni, and Jenna's heart stopped.

"No. That was something else."

"Behind the trees? Did Jenna—"

"No. Stop, Toni."

"Jonathan? You mean Dad? What are you talking about?"

"Focus, Jenna. Listen to what I'm saying to you. God has tried to wipe this town out twenty-seven times."

"I find that hard to believe," said Toni. "Last I heard, God knew how to use a flood."

"That was for everything. This is about a single town."

Why did Mom ask about Daddy, Jenna asked her grandmother through their mental connection.

It was a mistake. A slip of the tongue. I need you to FOCUS!

Jenna shook her head. Her grandmother's voice had seared her mind as if she'd bitten into a scoop of ice cream.

"They're just floods, Mom. They happen. Isn't the town flanked by two rivers? It's in a valley for Christ's sake. It's a horrible location. That doesn't make it God's personal mission to destroy it."

"And the dead in the woods? Is that just poor location as well?"

"I don't know what that is. Maybe you're on strong meds and you're passing them onto your granddaughter through osmosis or something."

"What about the fact your daughter can see, wiseass?"

"That I don't need an explanation for. I can just be happy about it."

Toni shot Jenna a warm smile.

"Hi, kiddo. It's nice to see you."

"You too, Mom."

"Moving on. The floods aren't the only thing God's tried. There have been several explosions. One killed eight young women in a warehouse. Another killed several men in another warehouse. There was one in a trailer that killed children. Is this starting to get through to you yet? All of this happened in... This. One. Town."

"Bad things happen every day. It doesn't make them biblical."

"There's an evil in this town dammit."

Jenna's grandmother pointed at one of the books on the bed.

"There. That one. It tells about the Centralia Massacre. On November 11th 1919. There was a parade to celebrate the end of World War I. At the end of the parade a group of veterans lined up outside this building where the Industrial Workers of the World would meet. There are a bunch of different versions of what happened, but the facts are that five men were gunned down in a scuffle that broke out between the two groups. Including the Sheriff. One of the IWW members, a Wesley Everest, was dragged out of the local jail and lynched off the side of Mellen Street Bridge. Are you really going to stand there and tell me that doesn't sound like some evil shit?"

"Mom, the language."

"Who cares about a curse word right now? I'm trying to tell you this town has something dark and horrible at its core. There's a reason the Push wanted me to move here, and for Jenna to come here now."

"Wait a minute. Are you even sick, Mom?" Asked Toni.

Grandman Marie looked away.

"Are you kidding me? You told me you were on your deathbed just to get us here? What the hell's wrong with you?"

Toni rushed over to Jenna. Fueled by her sudden rage, she gripped her daughter's free wrist and yanked her away from her grandmother. Everything went black. Jenna stumbled over one of her grandmother's stacks of books and fell hard to the floor.

"Jenna! I'm so sorry, sweetie."

"Mom, I can't see. I'm blind again."

Jenna wanted to cry. She was terrified and overwhelming sadness ripped through her chest. She never imagined she'd be able to see again. It'd been a miracle, and now that miracle was ripped away from her. She lost her sight all over again. Feelings she managed to repress flooded her mind. She couldn't breathe.

"Jenna, babygirl, breathe. Calm down. You have to relax and take a breath."

Jenna felt her mother's hands on the sides of her face. Then one moved to her chest.

"Breathe, sweetie."

But Jenna's lungs wouldn't work. Her entire body had shut down. She'd had everything back. Her future. Her friends. Finally, she had hope. Only to be thrust back into darkness. It was too much.

"No! Don't touch her. We're leaving. I won't put her through your bullshit," Toni said to her mother.

"Stop being so stubborn. Let me help her. She's turning blue."

"And what happens when you let go again? Do you plan on holding her hand everyday for the rest of her life? Every time she goes to school? Every date? Hell, every time she goes to the bathroom? Don't you get it? It'll be like an addiction. She'll go through this every time you let go, and it'll only get worse over time. What about when you do die, and your touch is gone forever? Then what?"

"She's already stronger than I ever could've imagined, Toni. The Push could heal her over time, or she could use it as another form of sight. All we can do is hope and try."

"No. I can't put her through that over and over again."

"Don't you think she deserves a vote?"

"She doesn't have a clue what's-"

Jenna took in a long painful gasp of air.

"Mom."

"Shush. Just keep breathing, pumpkin. Deep. In and out."

"I wanna see. I know it's not forever. But for now. Please."

"Jenna, it'll only get harder for you."

"I get it. I mean, I know how much it'll hurt, but I'd rather have five more minutes than nothing at all."

"If that's what you truly want, I won't stand in your way, but I can't promise I'll be able to comfort you in the aftermath. Words won't ease your pain."

"I get it. It's worth the risk."

The floor creaked behind her and seconds later the book-filled room was on full display again. Her chest relaxed and sweet air filled her lungs. The tension and grief that locked down her entire body was gone. She could repress the dark thoughts again. Bury them under her current excitement.

"I want to read all of your books, Grandma. I miss it so much."

"You have your audiobooks, sweetie."

"And they're great. It's just not the same as the voices in my head when I read them."

"There won't be any books to read if we don't save this town first," said her grandmother.

"But how do we save a whole town, Grandma? Evacuate everyone?"

"That'll save lives but it won't solve the problem. The evil will still exist. Even the floods and fires couldn't wash it away."

"Then what're you suggesting, Mom? How do we defeat an evil that God apparently can't?"

"We do what God can't. We face it head on."

"I can't believe these words are coming out of my mouth, but what does evil look like? Where do we find it? Google Maps? Is it Bigfoot? What logical plan could you really have?" asked Toni.

"I've searched every nook and cranny in this town."

"What's a cranny?" asked Jenna.

"It's short for cranberry, sweetie. That saying's never made sense to me. It's like a slogan for English muffins or something," replied Toni.

"None of that is right, Toni. Is this the type of nonsense you teach my granddaughter?"

"That's how Dad explained it to me, Mom."

"That makes sense. Your father was a touch of eat-the-paste kinda special."

"Nice. Way to paint a picture for Jenna."

"I already knew Grandpa was kinda… slow."

"Et tu Brute?"

"What?"

"Are you kidding me? Julius Caesar? How have you not learned about Ancient Rome? Remind me to have a word with your teachers."

"Mom, I'm homeschooled. You're literally my only teacher."

"Way to put your own mother on blast, pumpkin."

"Moving on! As I was saying, I've searched everywhere and the only place that made my hair stand up was under the Mellen Street Bridge."

"Where that bad guy was hung?"

"Hanged, honey."

"That doesn't sound right," said Jenna.

"Pretty sure, sweetie."

"I wish someone would hang me right now so I wouldn't have to deal with you two," said the grandmother.

"That escalated quickly, Mom."

"That's really dark, Grandma."

Her grandmother pinched the bridge of her nose and Jenna couldn't help but think… *this is what I've been missing all this time. This is what it's like to have a grandmother. For all of us to be together. Driving each other crazy. I love it.*

Jenna's grandmother looked over at her and gave her a wide soft smile. It was the first smile she'd ever seen that actually reached her grandmother's eyes. The only time she'd ever seen her genuinely happy. It didn't last long though as her grandmother returned to the task at hand.

"I think there's a reason they chose to hang that man off that bridge. I don't think it was just a lynching. I think it was a sacrifice to whatever lives under that bridge."

"So you think it's some goat-eating troll? Like in the nursery rhymes or folk tales?"

"Not a troll, no, but most folk tales have a root of truth to them. There's something under that bridge. I felt its presence, but I'm too old to find its gate or door. My Push has started to fade."

Her grandmother moved to a nearby mirror and looked into Jenna's eyes through her own.

"What is that? You keep saying your Push, My Push, Mom's Push, but you haven't said what it is."

"The women in our family have been blessed with powers of the mind, Jenna. We can move things. Connect to people like I've connected with you. It's a gift, but it can also be a weapon."

"I don't understand."

Jenna turned to her mother.

"Is this true?"

"Yes, but-

"Why didn't you tell me? I've been struggling so much since the accident, and I have powers that could've helped? What the hell, Mom?!"

"It's only helpful if you can see what you're moving, sweetie."

"I could've used your eyes," Jenna said before turning to her grandmother. "Right?"

Toni reached over and took her daughter's free hand.

"Can you feel me? My thoughts in your mind? It'd feel like lightning bolts firing off between our brains."

"Like what you and I are feeling, Jenna," said her grandmother. "But weaker."

"No. I don't feel anything. B-but I don't understand. You said I can connect with other people."

"Other people with the Push."

"But you said all of the women-"

"Your mother turned her back on it. Her power faded to nothing."

"I barely feel anything anymore, pumpkin. I'm sorry."

Jenna pulled her hand from her mother's grasp.

"I can't believe you kept this from me. You had no right."

"I'm your mother. I'm the ONLY one with the right to make any decisions regarding what I expose you to or not."

"Whatever. How am I supposed to help you fight this evil, Grandma? I just found out I even have these powers. I don't have the first clue how to use them."

"I'll teach you, and then we go. It isn't hard. You need to learn how to focus. Your power is strong. Raw but mighty. Together, we can find the door, and I can show you how to defeat the evil inside."

"That's insane. She's a child, Mom."

"And do you remember how powerful YOU were at her age? Before you turned your back on it?"

"What happens if this thing separates you two? You're a frail old woman with faded power and she's blind without your touch. What then?"

"That's why you're coming with us."

"Because THAT sounds like something I'd do. I'm the one that didn't want to have anything to do with the Push, remember? I can't let Jenna go on a suicide mission. Even if I don't believe this evil thing exists. What kind've mother would I be?"

"You'd be the kind that let your daughter save a few thousand lives."

"That's a great sentiment, but let's get real here. None of these people are Jenna's responsibility, and my only responsibility is my daughter."

"I can't just let people die, Mom. If Grandma really thinks we can save them, don't we have to? What kind of people would we be if we don't even try?"

Toni stood in silence for what felt like forever. They all looked up as thunder rolled above their heads. A massive streak of lightning illuminated the world outside the bedroom's windows. Cracka-BOOM! All three women jumped.

"It's starting, Toni. We don't have much time. It won't take much rain to make those rivers breach their banks."

"C'mon, Mom. What would David Bowie say?" said Jenna.

Toni smiled. She couldn't help herself.

"He'd say we could be heroes. Just for one day."

***

An hour later, all three women stood on the bridge and looked over the railing at the raging Chehalis River below. The water was already threatening to flood the banks on either side. The bridge itself was the length of a football field. It was two lanes wide and the torrential rain had turned the gray asphalt to a jet black.

"We have to get down there before the water gets too high," said Jenna's grandmother.

"What happens if it gets too high once we're through the gate, or door, or whatever?" said Toni.

Jenna was interested in the answer to that particular question as well. Her grandmother ignored it.

"C'mon!" yelled Grandma Marie..

Jerked to her right, Jenna found herself dragged to the nearest end of the bridge by her grandmother. Toni was on their heels, fuming about her mother's lack of answers. They stepped into the grass and surveyed the steep bank in front of them.

"If we get separated, stay put. I'll come back to you," said her grandmother.

Jenna nodded. Her entire body shook from a combination of fear and excitement. Learning how to use her powers was both exhilarating and exhausting. It felt like her grandmother had tried to jam generations of knowledge into an hour of practice.

It took half an hour for her to turn a single page of one book. Her grandmother just kept saying focus, focus, focus like some eye-doctor's mantra. Jenna squinted, pointed, waved her hands stupidly, and yet the book wouldn't move. Not even a little bit. She even tried Hermione's Levioso spell. No go.

"Clear your mind. Stop with the staring and the squinting. You're seeing it through my eyes, remember? And no waving. This isn't a parlor trick. See the book where you want it to be. Believe that's where the book should be, and then move it there."

Jenna shook her entire body, cleared her thoughts, and looked at the book. Magic was real. She could see through her grandmother's eyes. That was proof enough, but no matter how much she focused the book wouldn't move.

She was about to give up until her mother and grandmother started going at it again. Much to her mother's disappointment, it was Jenna's desire to make them stop fighting that finally drove her to turn all of her emotion toward moving the book. She knew slamming the book against the far wall would make them stop. She screamed out with her mind for them to quit fighting and the book soared across the room. It slammed into one of the bookcases. Several books fell to the floor with a series of heavy thuds. Her mother and grandmother stopped arguing and Toni lowered her head in defeat.

"It looks like you're as ready as you're going to be," said her grandmother.

As she made her way down the steep bank behind her grandmother, Jenna wondered if she could duplicate the same emotion she felt back at the house.

"Do you feel it, Jenna?" asked Grandma Marie.

Jenna didn't answer, but she did feel the power of the door. There was a sort of energy in the soles of her feet. Like she was walking on hot coals.

"We're close."

"I don't see anything, Mom," said Toni.

"If you could see it, it wouldn't be hidden. It's a feeling. Jenna knows what I'm talking about."

"Is that true, sweetie?"

"I think so. There's something here."

They reached the river and tightroped their way towards the bridge as the water roared past in front of them.

If I fall in, I'll definitely drown, thought Jenna.

I wouldn't let that happen, thought her grandmother.

The bridge was twenty feet away when Jenna was forced to stop. A burst of energy slammed into her as if a heavy metal door slammed in her face.

"Grandma? What's going on?"

"We're nearly there. We have to Push through it."

Jenna and her grandmother tightened their grip, and Jenna reached back for her mother's hand. Toni took it. It was a hollow hold compared to the electricity that coursed between Jenna and her grandmother. She couldn't help but wish her mother still had the Push. She'd give anything to have the same intimate mental connection with her.

Stepping forward, Jenna felt as if she'd breached some invisible wall. It was like stepping outside into the blazing shine of a low sun after months in the dark. Warmth washed over her, and she couldn't understand how something evil could make her feel so good.

"This doesn't feel like there's evil nearby, Grandma."

"Evil doesn't draw people to it with pain or sadness. It promises them the greatest things in life: wealth, love, happiness. It spills honey in your ears as it bleeds you from your wrists. When we open its doorway, you'll feel the darkness. We're here to kill it. When it knows… that's when it'll show its true colors."

"I think-"

Toni started to say before she stepped on a loose stone and twisted her ankle. She lost her balance and toppled into the river. Jenna nearly lost her grip on her mother's hand, but instinct made her clamp down with her fingers, tightening around Toni's palm like a vice.

"Mom!"

The intense current pulled on Toni as she struggled against it. Jenna's sneakers skidded on the wet grass as she was dragged towards the river's edge. Her grandmother tightened her grip around Jenna's hand and she felt as if every tiny bone in her palm would snap. Her toes were suddenly cold as the front of her shoes were submerged beneath the rushing water. The river threatened to pull her mother into its depths. Toni was completely submerged. All that remained above the dirty brown surface was the arm Jenna had a hold of.

"She can't breathe, Grandma!"

"I can't pull her free alone, Jenna. We have to do this together."

Jenna tried to focus on her mother, but a voice in her head stole her breath away.

I love you, Jenna. Goodbye, sweetie.

Mom? I hear you!

I'll never leave you, babygirl. Know that.

No!

"NO!"

Jenna closed her eyes and focused on what she could see through her grandmother's. Her mother was there, just beneath the surface. The vision was blurred and Jenna realized her grandmother was crying.

"Toni, swim goddammit!"

Tell grandma, I've never hated her. She's always been my hero.

You'll tell her yourself, Mom. I'm not letting you go.

Jenna screamed at the top of her lungs as she pictured her mother soaring out of the water and landing on the shore.

"Give me my mother!"

Toni burst out of the water. She flew over Jenna's head and slammed down on the bank behind her. She coughed out what seemed like a gallon of water as Jenna scrambled to her. She let go of her grandmother's hand and everything went black again as she dove on top of Toni. She gripped her in a bear hug with her head against her mother's soaked chest. Toni continued to cough and gasp for air.

"I can't breathe, Jenna."

"Call me sweetie. Call me pumpkin. Call me anything you want. I don't care."

"Um okay. I didn't know that was a problem before."

"It doesn't matter."

"Are you okay, Toni?"

"Yes, Mom. I think so. Once my daughter stops trying to crack all of my ribs."

Jenna relaxed and sat up, reaching out blindly for her grandmother's hand. The older woman took it, causing Toni to come back into view. She was soaked and exhausted, but otherwise okay.

"Mom. I heard you. In my head."

"I heard you too."

"What are you two talking about?"

"Mom said goodbye with her thoughts. She still has some of the Push."

"I didn't think that was possible," said her grandmother.

"I don't feel it anymore. I think it was just in the moment. Like a last rush of power before… you know."

"Let's end this evil and get you back home. But if your power is gone for good, you'd better stay here. My heart won't take another close call like that one," said her grandmother.

"No way. Forget it. I'm not letting you and Jenna go in alone."

"Please, Mom. Grandma is right. There's no way I'll be able to focus on killing it if I have to worry about you."

Toni shook her head and looked into her mother's face.

"Can you see me, Jenna?"

"Yes."

"If you feel like you can't do it you get the hell out of there and back to me. You don't owe this town anything. Do you hear me?"

"Yes."

Toni sat up and took Jenna in her arms. They hugged each other for what felt like an eternity until Toni finally let go.

"We'll be right back, Mom."

"You'd better be, or I'm coming in after you, babygirl."

And with that said, Jenna's grandmother started to lead her back towards the bridge.

"Mom," said Toni.

"Yes?"

"You've got my entire world in your hands."

"I know it."

Jenna gave her mother one last wave and followed her grandmother back along the shore. The river had engulfed much of the bank as they tended to Toni, and there was very little room to maneuver. They made their way around a curve in the bank, and Toni was taken out of view.

The energy of the thing beneath the bridge was palpable. Any lingering doubts Jenna might have had about the thing's existence were obliterated. They reached the place where the bridge cut through the shore and stopped.

"It's here," said her grandmother.

"It just looks like regular dirt and grass."

"It's beneath that. You have to picture it there below the surface."

"How? I have no idea what it is or what it'd even look like. How can I picture something I've never seen?"

"I don't think it's any one specific door or gate. I think it'll take on the shape we give it. It's just energy. We have to shape it."

"Okay. How?"

"Do you remember the storm doors that lead into my basement?"

Jenna remembered them very well. They were two metal doors that seemed to lead directly into the ground. They were painted a dull matted gray, and she could see the spots of dark maroon rust beneath the single coat of paint. She used to use the doors as a slide for her toys. The groove between them was perfect for rolling a ball up and down.

"Yes, I remember them."

"Good. Picture those doors here. Right in front of us, leading into the ground."

Jenna pictured the doors, paint, rust, and groove, then stood in shock as the doors materialized in the river bank.

"Holy shit," said Jenna.

"Let's not tell your mother about that particular slip."

"Deal."

Her grandmother reached for the groove in the center of the storm doors, placed her fingers around the metal curve of the right door, and lifted. She opened it wide and heat blasted them in the face. It reeked of five-day old sun-baked roadkill. Jenna turned away, burying her nose in the crook of one arm. The energy that had warmed her like a winter bonfire now froze her to her core. The hair on her arms stood on end as goose flesh covered her entire body.

"It's so hot inside but I'm freezing," said Jenna.

"It means to confuse us. It's defending itself. Imagine you're surrounded by a shield of warm energy. It'll combat the cold."

"Okay."

Jenna imagined a force field of yellow just above her skin. She pictured the sun filling it with heat like solar panels. It flowed and pulsed with energy.

"I think I'm ready, Grandma."

"Let's go end this then."

Her grandmother lifted the other storm door open and they stepped into the pitch-black home of Centralia's evil.

***

The horrid acrid roadkill smell only worsened with each step.

"Don't let go of my hand, Jenna. No telling how many twists and turns are down here. Take small steps too. The ground could drop off at any second and I can't even see the end of my nose."

That's how I've been living every day, thought Jenna.

I didn't mean to be insensitive.

I didn't take it like that. Just stating facts. This feels pretty natural to me. I hate the darkness, but I'm not afraid of it.

Can you smell anything that might give us a sense of direction?

No. All I smell is rotten flesh and it's everywhere.

What about your ears? Do you hear anything?

Give me a second.

They stopped, and Jenna strained to hear even the slightest sound. When she did, it shook her. There, somewhere in the darkness, was the sound of something dragging towards them. No, that was wrong. It wasn't something. It was many things. She pictured what approached them from the pitch black, using one of her heightened senses to paint a horrific picture.

There, that was the sound of a foot scraping through dirt, shifting rocks and pebbles. That was the sound of someone clawing at dirt, like a dog digging for a bone. There was the click of a jaw as it opened and closed. The gnashing of teeth. The shifting of weight on loose gravel.

There are things coming.

From where, Jenna?

Everywhere.

I'm going to give us some light. You MUST be ready for anything. If something attacks hurl them against the wall, tear their limbs off, whatever you have to do to defend yourself. The only limit to your power is your own self-doubt. Are you ready?

I- Yes.

Her grandmother reaffirmed her grip on Jenna's arm, and then Jenna heard the flick of a lighter. She saw a tiny flame ignite like a single star in the center of a black hole. The flame expanded to the size of a basketball and flew into the darkness in front of them. The tunnel was tighter than Jenna pictured and it was filled wall to wall with Centralia's dead.

There were the same ash-skinned and drowned from behind the trees, but they were joined by others. Some were missing limbs, while flesh melted off the bones of others. One woman had no head. Jenna knew they weren't zombies but she couldn't help thinking of *Dawn of the Dead.*

Most of the dead limped or shuffled towards them, but there were several that were forced to drag themselves across the tunnel's floor.

That must've been the digging that I heard, she thought.

"Pick your targets. We can't let them get any closer. There are too many. They'll overwhelm us."

Jenna focused on the group closest to her side of the tunnel.

"Should we just split them down the middle?"

"That's fine. Just put them down for good."

Jenna jerked her head and snapped the legs of the dead at the front of the crowd. They fell but kept coming. She then broke the neck of one that'd reached her feet. CRACK! The sound echoed down the tunnel as the thing with the broken neck continued to reach for her.

"How do we kill what's already dead?"

"You rip them apart."

As if to give an example, Grandma Marie lifted one of the things in the air with her mind and yanked it apart at each joint. Blood like black ichor sprayed across the other dead.

"I don't know if I can do that. They were people."

"WERE people. They're something dark now and if you don't destroy it, it'll kill us without a second's hesitation."

Jenna looked down at the thing at her feet. She felt sorry for it and the hesitation cost her. It reached out and grabbed her ankle. Searing pain erupted where the thing gripped her. The pain forced her into action. She ripped the thing's arm off at the shoulder and yanked its dead hand from her ankle. She then used her newfound powers to lift its body, then hurled it at the rest of the approaching dead.

Looking down at her leg, Jenna saw that it was raw and red in the shape of a hand. The thing burned her badly. The wound seared and every slight brush of hot air made her want to scream. It felt as if the dead still had a hold of her. Her imaginary shield of warmth was gone, and the freezing cold of the dark energy within the tunnel was like a smack across her face.

Her grandmother tore one dead thing apart after another with relative ease. Black blood and yellow puss sprayed everywhere as rotted body parts sailed through the air.

"I can't keep this up too much longer, Jenna. I need your help."

Jenna did her best to ignore the pain in her leg and focused on the task at hand. The dead on the side of her tunnel were nearly upon them. If her and her grandmother died, it would be her fault.

One after another she tore limbs and heads off of the things with a simple thought. A sound like ripping a drumstick off of turkey filled the tunnel. Once she'd regained her focus and stopped thinking of the things as people, tearing them apart got easier. They were nearly through them all when her grandmother suddenly collapsed onto one knee.

"That's it. That's all I've got."

"You said our only limitations are our own minds. Were you lying?"

"Of course not."

"Then get up and help me."

"I can't. I wasn't lying to your mother just to get you two here. I really am dying, Jenna. I'm too weak. I've got nothing left here."

Jenna didn't know how to take in what her grandmother said without completely abandoning her attack on the dead. She could only deal with one major issue at a time. Her grandmother might be dying, but if she let the dead reach them, they'd both be dead anyway. She stepped in front of her weakened grandmother.

"You rest, Grandma. I'll finish them off."

She held arms out in front of her as her grandmother gripped Jenna's ankle to maintain their connection. Holding her arms out was theatre. Jenna knew it. She didn't need her arms to do what she had to, but it made her feel stronger. She had no idea why. Using her arms like a conductor's baton, she slammed the things against the tunnel's walls and ceilings until they were nothing but shattered bones covered in dead skin. Jenna dispatched the final member of Centralia's dead seconds before her grandmother let her go.

Jenna was in the dark.

"Grandma?"

"I'm here, Jenna."

Jenna reached out for her grandmother and heard the woman step back to avoid her.

"What are you doing? I can't see."

"I know. I don't want you in my head for this part."

"What do you mean? I don't understand."

"I had to know how strong you were. Had to see it with my own eyes. Sacrificing the dead was the only way."

"Sacrificing what? What're you talking about? Please take my hand. There may be more."

"They won't hurt you anymore."

"How do you know that?"

"Because I'm their puppet master. I made them attack us. I had to see what you can do. Make sure your mind is strong enough."

"You're not making any sense. Why would you make them attack us? What's my mind gotta be strong enough for?"

"To hold my power when I take over. My body's dying, Jenna, but my mind doesn't have to."

"I don't understand."

"I've been trying to move into your head for years. I always thought it was your mother that placed defenses in my way, and the pain that kept you away was from me trying to break through. It turns out you were the one defending yourself all along. You were already powerful then, and you didn't even know about the Push."

"You were hurting me on purpose the whole time?"

"It should've been painless. I should've just been able to slip in and lock you away in a dark corner of your own mind."

"How could you? You're my grandmother!"

"Because I made a promise to a very evil creature a long time ago that I'd watch over this gateway to his realm until the time came."

Jenna turned and felt for the closest way out. She needed to get away from her grandmother. The old woman was either evil or insane, and neither meant good news for her.

"Time came for what?" asked Jenna to keep her grandmother talking.

Did she let the flame go out? Are we both in the dark, thought Jenna.

"The time for every gate in every Centralia around the world to open, and let his great army rise."

"You're sick, Grandma. We need to get Mom. You need help."

"No. I'll be fine. You're powerful, but you won't be able to fight me this time. Not after all of the energy you've just exerted."

"Screw that. We're leaving. Me and Mom. We're going home, and leaving you here to die."

"Leaving me? You can't even make it out of this cave on your own. And this wouldn't be the first time I died in Centralia, Jenna. It won't even be the second. He keeps bringing me back because I have to fulfill my promise. It's why we have the Push in the first place."

"No! I refuse to believe this was all a trap."

"I tried to bring you here once before."

Images started playing in Jenna's mind like an old family video as her grandmother explained. She was in the backseat of a car as her father drove. They sang along with a Taylor Swift song. They were happy. Indestructible.

A woman stepped into the path of their headlights and her father was forced to jerk the car to the left. It flew into the woods, flipping over and over again. Jenna watched her father from the backseat as he slammed his head into the driver's side window. She didn't know the impact had knocked him unconscious. Glass shattered and sprayed back on Jenna. The car slammed into something big and stopped at once. Jenna's head was jerked back into the rear window, cracking the thick glass. Her eyes rolled back as she blacked out.

"Someone was there, on the road. Daddy had to swerve to miss them."

"I tricked your father into driving here, forced you two into the crash that left you blind."

"I don't believe you. No one could do that to their own family."

"Your father wasn't my family, and dead or alive you'd serve my needs."

Jenna stumbled over a rock and fell hard to her knees. She started to crawl. It was safer. She didn't care how ridiculous she might look to her grandmother if the fire was still lit. All she knew was that she had to get out of that cave. It wasn't because of the dead things, or even the fear of the gate that threatened to overwhelm her. It was her grandmother's words. They hurt far more than the burn on her leg ever could, and she didn't want to hear anymore.

"I should've killed your father then, but I figured his injuries would do him in. I took you from the twisted metal and brought you here. He followed us, and shot me. I mortally wounded him before I blacked out. A gut wound. A slow death. He managed to get you to a hospital, and then returned to finish me off. I killed him instead."

"Why? He loved you. We all did. Why would you hurt us?"

"I've already told you. Evil gives us anything we want. Love, money, happiness. Your mother abandoned me for you and your father. She rejected me after I told her about her power. The evil here in Centralia was all I had left."

Jenna screamed as her grandmother gripped her wrist hard enough to bring her to her knees. The pain was excruciating, but she could see again. The mouth of the cave wasn't as far away as she thought. Slowly, she managed to get to her feet.

"My last bit of advice… give yourself to it. There are places like this all across the country and they're all epicenters of evil. One has burned with his flame for over sixty years. Good can't win. Accept that and through me, you'll stand at his side."

The fight for Jenna's mind had begun. Her head felt as if it'd split in two. There was pain and pressure. Her mind felt crowded. There were suddenly too many thoughts. The whispers of the dead things bounced around her skull as her grandmother tried to coax her into submission.

Give in. You will exist for all eternity.

Never!

We can all be together. Me, you, and your mother. We can be happy.

I won't let you near her!

I've had enough of this!

Jenna felt her mind go fuzzy. She couldn't focus. Darkness started to creep into her thoughts.

Let me in or I'll destroy you and kill your mother once I'm done.

That was too much. Her grandmother stole her father from her. She wouldn't let her hurt her mother too.

"Get off of me!"

Jenna unleashed all of her pain and anger on her grandmother. The betrayal devastated her. Her grandmother had killed her father. Her dear sweet father.

"I hate you!" She yelled as she lashed out with her mind, breaking her grandmother's hold, and sending herself into darkness once again.

She couldn't see her grandmother but she knew she'd lifted the old woman into the air. Jenna could feel the shift in the space around her.

"Go to Hell, Grandma."

She cast her grandmother deep into the endless darkness, and heard her screams echo through the tunnel.

Dropping to her knees, Jenna began to sob. She might've just killed her own grandmother. A woman she loved that admitted to murdering her father, and tried to lock her away in her own mind. How was she supposed to make sense of all of that? How would she tell her mother?

Booming laughter filled the tunnel. Jenna couldn't see what was coming but somehow knew there was a fiery orange glow heading her way, igniting the tunnel in hellfire as it came.

"YOU ARE POWERFUL, YOUNG ONE. FAR MORE POWERFUL THAN YOUR GRANDMOTHER."

The dark voice vibrated deep in her bones. She didn't hear it so much as felt it.

"Leave me alone. Please."

"YOU WILL BE A GODDESS IN MY MASTER'S ARMY. A LEADER IN THE COMING WAR FOR YOUR REALM."

She had to leave. If the thing reached her, she'd never feel the warmth of the sun again. She was sure of it. But she couldn't see. The blindness was upon her for good now, and without her grandmother's eyes she had no idea which way was out.

"Hello, Jenna."

Wait. She knew that voice.

"I want you to listen to me."

"Daddy?"

"That's right. It's me, Jenna."

Her father was there with her, whispering into her ear with his sweet voice. The one that always made her feel better.

"I need you to stand up and move."

"But I can't see, Daddy."

"Hold out your hands."

Jenna held her hands out, palms up.

"I'm sorry, Jenna. I know it's awful, but it's the only way to save you."

Something was placed in each of Jenna's hands. They were round, soft, and slimy. The second they touched her skin she could see the orange glow she imagined. It WAS real and it was filling the tunnel all around her. But she saw her father too, and her heart nearly burst with joy.

His face was withdrawn, his blue eyes were a lifeless gray, and he was horribly thin, but it was him. He was real.

"Be careful with those, Jenna."

"I don't understand, Daddy?"

"They're your grandmother's eyes. I stole them from her. They're yours now. Keep them if you want. Use them. Or destroy them. That's entirely up to you, but use them now. Get out of here, Jenna."

Jenna ignored the fact she had her grandmother's eyes in her hands. She made sure not to squeeze them. The idea of crushing them in her fists made her stomach lurch.

"THE GIRL IS MY MASTER'S PRIZE, SPIRIT. IT IS HER FATE."

"Don't listen to it, Jenna. Just go."

"But I can't leave you."

"I'm already gone. I'm just a shadow here. One of Centralia's many. But every time you think of me, I'll be with you."

"Daddy?"

"Go and when you get out destroy this tunnel. Bring it all crashing down, and save this town."

"YOU PUT TOO MUCH HOPE IN THE HANDS OF A CHILD."

"Your voice trembles as you say that, Demon. You and I both know how strong she is."

"Is it true? About the other Centralias? Are they evil too?"

"Yes, but there are other people fighting those evils, and if there are Centralias without heroes find them, and save those poor people. They need you. This thing can't be allowed to bring its army to the surface."

"I'll try. I promise."

"Tell your mother I love her."

"I love you, Daddy."

"I love you too, Jenna. Now hold those eyes up high and get the hell out of here. Go!"

Jenna held up her grandmother's eyes and saw the full glow of the approaching Demon for the first time. It was a fierce light that burned at the walls of the tunnel and there in the center was the silhouette of a massive Demon. It had to duck in order to keep its long horns from scraping the tunnel's ceiling. Its broad shoulders dug into the arch of the tunnel on both sides, knocking stone and dirt into its path.

"COME, CHILD. HERE IS WHERE YOU'LL FIND YOUR TRUE POTENTIAL."

She turned from the approaching Demon and ran for the exit, leaving her father behind her. Leaping over Centralia's dead, she rushed toward the sunlight that seemed miles away from her.

"YOU CANNOT ESCAPE ME. TURN. TURN AND EMBRACE YOUR MASTER."

Jenna pushed herself to run harder than she'd ever run before. Her lungs burned from the effort and the heat within the tunnel. Salty sweat stung her eyes as it coated her face. The sunlight inched closer and closer but so did the glow of the hellfire behind her. She swore she felt the Demon's breath on her back, hot and heavy. It was right behind her. She knew it was real, and as the mouth of the tunnel grew close enough to give her hope, her heart broke at the sight of the storm doors closing. First one. Then the other. They blocked out the sun with the echo of metal on metal.

"No!"

She ran at them at full speed and willed them open. They were feet away now. She wouldn't be able to slow down. She'd slam into them and then the Demon would have her.

"I said OPEN!"

She tucked her hands against her chest to protect her grandmother's eyes from the impending impact. Blind, she turned her shoulder towards the metal doors and prepared for a lot of pain. Something brushed through her hair.

The Demon's hand?

And then she was covered in sunlight. She landed on the bank of the river. Rain continued to pour down and the river had risen halfway up the bank. She lifted her grandmother's eyes toward the open storm doors and saw that the Demon was nearly upon her..

Scrambling to her feet, Jenna forced all of her emotion into one thought.

Close the Gate. Bring this bitch down.

Sheer energy radiated from every pore. She felt as if electricity was coursing through her body. The ground shook beneath her feet and the storm doors fell back into the mouth of the tunnel.

"NO!"

The Demon's yell was cut off as the tunnel began to cave in. The bank disappeared in front of her as it collapsed in on itself. The bridge to her right shifted and the end fell into the river. Jenna stumbled backwards, gripping her grandmother's eyes in her hands as tight as she dared, certain she was about to fall blindly into the raging river behind her.

"Gotcha," said Toni as she grabbed Jenna by the waist.

They scrambled up the remaining bank before it too disappeared into a massive sinkhole. Toni guided Jenna onto the road, wondering why her daughter refused to open her hands. Once on the safety of the road, Toni watched and Jenna listened as the bank continued to swallow itself.

It was several minutes before the cave-in finished. Toni stared in disbelief at the devastation. The rain stopped and the sun broke through the clouds. The river slowed and subsided. There would be no flood that day.

"Your grandmother?"

Jenna shook her head.

Toni lowered her head. She started to cry.

"Mom."

Toni looked up. Jenna opened her hands, revealing her grandmother's eyes.

"There's a lot I have to tell you on the ride home. Can you please leave the radio off?"

RICHAR

WNEE

ROCK

Nemaha

X | X! | X!! | X!!! | X!V

LINE

Clearcreek

Bern

St. Bridget

I'D

Berv

St. Benedict

Sabetha

Oneida

ID.

Price

N.

GD.

Baileyville

Fair

ell

Cedar

Seneca

Capioma

North Fork

Woodlawn

NEMAHA

Kelly

PAC.

Centralia

Granada

River

PAC.

Muddy

R.

eits or

W.

Goff

s P.O.

Corning

val

Wetmore

Bancroft

Neta

PAC.

Neuchatel

America.
City

Savannah

Ontario

St.

PAC.

Circle

uth

Qua

Gold

www.MyGenealogyHounds.com

Sundown

Michael Patrick Hicks

Centralia, KS

Location of Centralia, Kansas

Coordinates: 39°43′27″N 96°7′52″W

Country   United States

State   Kansas

County   Nemaha

Area

• Total   0.45 sq mi (1.17 km2)

Population

• Total   512

First Epicenter Sighting

• January 1978

Percent Burn

• 41%

Hannah Ford could feel the stares on her back, her sides, all around her. She sipped her coffee, then turned on her countertop stool, slowly, deliberately, to meet the glares of her watchers head on. Instead, she found hurriedly averted gazes as heads turned away to study other, less interesting, facets of the diner. Six others were in the diner with her, all white, and while she had felt them observing her seconds ago only a few had the temerity to meet her head on now. She met the eyes of those bold enough to look at her head on and refused to look away first. She stared them down, coolly, sipping her coffee, one elbow propped up on the counter behind her.

"Morning," she said. The white man nodded, his lips a thin line, but said nothing in return. He held her stare a moment longer to save face, then turned his attention to the menu.

One of her other observers was quickly typing out a text on his cell phone. These men had been brave enough to stare her down when her back was turned, but each lost their courage in the time it took her to complete one revolution. They looked away, red-faced, one by one.

Hannah wondered if any of them had the nerve to rope themselves a young black boy named Harlan Reynolds, hitch him to their pick-up truck, and drag him through a mile of rocky fields to the Centralia Cemetery and the hanging tree he'd been strung from. Most of these men were middle-aged, but not exactly fit. Still, it was possible she was sitting among some tired-looking, pot-bellied murderers. A few were older, approaching retirement age, and it felt safe to rule them out, but only tentatively. The 80-year-old with thinning hair looked awfully spry, and she couldn't help but chuckle to herself at that.

Reynolds' demise had been, incredulously, ruled a suicide, until parties unknown leaked the coroner's report detailing the extent of the damage inflicted upon Reynolds prior to being lynched. The public outcry was sufficient to force the Nemaha County Sheriff's office to reopen the case, "in light of these additional details," promising a complete and thorough investigation. The leaked reports pointing toward an attempted cover-up made Hannah's blood boil, for so many reasons. She suspected, too, that the promise of a deeper investigation was nothing more than lip service given the nationwide attention the case had received following the leak. In the two months since Reynolds's death, though, the news hadn't even bothered to follow-up and report on the sheriff's supposed investigation, and no arrests had been made. For all intents and purposes, Reynolds was just another dead and forgotten Black man, lost in the shuffle of bigger headlines to captivate a nation's short attention span.

And yet, that wasn't why Hannah had come to Centralia, Kansas. Not entirely, anyway. Odds were, she would have been quietly stewing over the news, or rather, lack of news, at home, alone and angry at the injustice, but content to let others get involved in her place. A lynching wasn't her usual type of business. Not exactly, anyway. The photos she found online changed all that.

She hadn't wanted to look at those images, although she had certainly seen worse in her days, but a morbid curiosity drew her attention. She felt responsible for bearing witness, to try and absorb some of the pain Harlan Reynolds had experienced in his last moments. Although Anonymous had leaked the photos all over social media and they had spread like wildfire from there, that wasn't where Hannah had first seen them. She first encountered the photos capturing Reynolds murder in a private occult group she had been a part of for a number of years now. The poster had been asking if anybody recognized the symbols in the tree trunk. The image had been cropped, in-camera most likely, and much of the carving was incomplete and out of frame. What was visible, though, was clearly arcane. The few responders didn't seem to know much about it, but promised to return when they had more information.

Hannah hadn't bothered to wait for updates. She'd packed her gear, loaded up her Jeep Wrangler, and made the twelve-hour drive from Ann Arbor, Michigan to Centralia, Kansas on little more than a whim. She didn't know what the cut-off symbols meant, but she knew the minute she saw them that this was her kind of job after all.

She finished her coffee, not expecting a refill from the disinterested waitress and not getting one, either. The waitress had been brusque from the start, pouring Hannah a single mug before finding something at the other end of the counter to busy herself with. Hannah set the empty cup down, left a few bills under the saucer, and stood. She turned around and nearly slammed into the wide, too-close, brown-shirted chest.

Her eyes roamed over the Nemaha County Sheriff patch on his sleeve, the badge on his chest, and a name tag that read MORELL, up to the hard, lined face staring down at her. He looked like he'd been carved from a hunk of granite, and his eyes were the coldest blue Hannah had ever seen.

"Sheriff," she said.

"Miss," he said. He stepped around her, taking a seat at the counter next to the one she'd been occupying. Sitting, they were nearly eye to eye. He looked her up and down, the toothpick between his lips bouncing. "What brings you to Centralia, you don't mind my asking?"

"Just passing through," she said.

"Well then, I hope you have a nice, quick visit."

Hannah nodded, and began to turn back to the door when his icy voice stopped her again.

"Word of advice, miss, if you'll allow it. You'll want to make sure you're out of town come sundown, you here? Folks round here, they don't take kindly to people like you come dark, you understand? They get skittish."

Hannah's blood went cold, and she nodded, stiffly. "Oh, I understand, Sheriff."

Centralia had been a sundown town back in the day, and Blacks had been prohibited from living within the town's borders. The laws might have officially been struck down, but attitudes were a lot harder to change. She knew of plenty of predominantly white cities and towns all across America where sundown policies were still in effect, even if only unofficially, and the police in those areas had little trouble coming up with various reasons for stopping a Black person. A broken taillight that mysteriously appeared as the officer made their way to the driver's side window of a Black man's car, flashlight swinging, or stopping somebody because 'they fit the description' of a supposed suspect.

The sheriff's warning, on top of Harlan Reynold's murder, was impossible to ignore. As was the fading sunlight.

She tucked her cellphone into the hip pocket of her blue jeans as she pushed through the diner's door. Her yellow Jeep was the most colorful thing around for miles, and as she approached, she saw the long slash of grey steel that cut its way from the gas cap up to the hood. Somebody had keyed her car while she'd been inside. Hannah shook her head and swore to herself, wondering if the sheriff had been responsible for this. Aside from Morell, nobody had come in or out of the diner during the time it had taken her to drink her one cup of coffee. Or maybe it had just been somebody offended by her Michigan license plate and the U of M faculty parking sticker in her windshield.

Walking around the Jeep, she studied her vehicle for any additional damage. Only the driver's side had been keyed, and the soft top was still secure. The doors were all locked, but she double-checked the cargo compartment to be sure. Her camera equipment was safe, and her small duffle bag with books, clothes, and toiletries didn't look like it had been disturbed.

Hannah checked her watch. Only a little more than twenty minutes until sundown. She had wanted to make it out to the Reynolds crime scene, but she also needed to find a place to bed down for the night. The tree would still be there in the morning, she decided, as she climbed into the Jeep and pointed the vehicle toward the town's borders.

Once she passed the quaint "YOU ARE NOW LEAVING CENTRALIA" sign, she said, "Hey, Siri, what's the nearest motel?"

***

Settled in her room, Hannah booted up her laptop and logged into the message board where she'd first learned about the Reynolds murder. She had saved the posted images but was curious to see if any new insights had been made since she'd last checked the prior evening.

As soon as the thread loaded, she was confronted with the crime scene photographs. The very first image at the top of the page showed Reynolds as discovered by the police, hanging from a tree in the town's cemetery, his arms limp at his sides and feet pointing lifelessly toward the short, scorched grass and headstones below.

The symbols that had been carved into the tree were barely discernible, but a second, low-resolution image showed them more plainly. The sigil had been carved high up the tree, and part of the top had been cut off in the photograph. Whatever eagle-eyed observer had originally spotted the carvings had cropped the image to better showcase the symbols. Unfortunately, it was so heavily cropped, and the carvings themselves were rather small, and an even smaller element of the photograph's larger composition, that it was difficult to make out much detail. To complicate matters further, at the time the photo had been taken the sun had cast a long, deep shadow from the tree's higher branches over the etchings. The cropped photo was hardly bigger than a thumbnail, and when blown-up to larger dimensions it was too much of a pixelated mess to make any sense of.

The only thing Hannah could read clearly about this image was the desperation in the OP's search for help: "Can anybody make any sense of what this says???"

What followed were the same unhelpful comments she'd seen last night. People telling the OP his image was too small, too illegible, and the shadows too dark to be readable. Others offered to help in any way they could but given the amount of digital artifacting in the low-resolution photos, the promises rang hollow.

Not for the first time, Hannah wished digital photography manipulation worked like it did on those TV crime shows, where you could crop and enhance, and pull out even the smallest details in the most brilliant ultra-high definition resolutions possible. Unfortunately, CSI was a fucking joke when it came to getting such details right and took an awful lot of dramatic liberties in order to shortcut reality for entertainment.

Less than twenty-four hours old, and the thread looked like it was already a dead topic. No new posts since last night. She sighed and put the laptop to sleep, not having really expected a different outcome than this. This was why she was in Centralia in the first place, to see those symbols firsthand, figure out what they meant, and why they were carved into a killing tree that a young black man had been lynched from. The fact that there were symbols carved into the tree bark at all was enough cause for concern, and it made the hair on the back of her neck stand on end. Although she had no idea what the symbols were, she could make out just enough in those deep black shadows to know it wasn't a simple John Loves Jane devotion. What she had seen was enough to send her into a twelve-hour drive across five states, and it made clear to her that the Reynolds murder, as heinous as it was, was not just a racially motivated killing. It was a ritualistic murder.

***

Hannah woke before her alarm, intent on getting an early start. What she thought of as her "normal life" as an academic allowed her a fairly flexible lifestyle, but she was accustomed to rising early, going to bed late, and operating on little sleep and a fairly high volume of caffeine. She figured she could kill the roughly two hours before sunrise in a local diner, reading over breakfast, before she crossed the city limits back into Centralia.

She was so eager to lay her eyes on the symbols carved into the hanging tree that she was tempted to skip breakfast and drive directly back into town. Her stomach rumbling and concern over what the Centralia locals might do if they saw a Black woman in their midst while it was still dark out was enough to dampen her enthusiasm. Besides that, she was very much looking forward to digging into the latest in John Connolly's Charlie Parker series, which she was enjoying and thought she might enjoy more alongside a plate of runny eggs and hash browns. Certainly, it would be more enjoyable than having the Nemaha County Sheriff sicced on her again, and she wasn't aiming to start her day off by getting arrested or worse. And she certainly wasn't planning on getting an eyeful of those symbols in such an up-close and personal manner as had befallen Harlan Reynolds, rest his soul.

Breakfast at a nearby diner was cheap and filling, and she was able to lose herself for a time in her Kindle. The coffee wasn't bad, not great by any stretch of the imagination, but the waitress was quick with the refills and with enough cream and sugar Hannah was able to drink four cups of the stuff without complaint. From her booth, she watched the sunrise through the clear glass window as she polished off the dinner plate-sized serving of hash browns, then read a couple more chapters over coffee to give the world some extra time to wake up for her.

Finally, bill paid, she unplanted herself, dropped the e-reader back in her purse, and pulled herself into the Wrangler. The morning sun was already warming the earth, promising to make life miserable with its heat as the day wore on. She was glad she'd already taken the soft top down, but if the heat kept up, she'd be putting it back on and blasting the AC soon enough.

Hannah was careful to observe the speed limit as she worked her way back into Centralia, crossing over the Black Vermillion River on Old Number 9. Farms and long stretches of cornfields eventually gave way to the small suburbs of the town proper, until the flat stretches of land, woods, and farms took hold again at Centralia's edges. At the northernmost edge was the cemetery where Reynolds had been murdered, but not buried. According to the news, his body had been interred a few miles away in his hometown of Seneca.

Reynolds had been discovered at the northern edge of Centralia Cemetery, where the graves were sparser and the land less heavily trafficked by visitors and mourners. The site of his demise was far enough removed from the heart of the cemetery that the four roads looping around the more central burial plots didn't even extend that far and the asphalt gave way to dirt well before reaching the hanging tree.

The Wrangler bounced over the rougher terrain of the narrower dirt road, but the cottonwood came into view soon enough.

She pulled to a stop and retrieved her camera gear from the cargo compartment in back. Although it had grown hotter in the short time it had taken her drive from the diner to the cemetery, a cold chill enveloped her as she stepped closer to the tree. Her breath bloomed before her in a smoky cloud and goose pimples rose across her arms. Cemeteries were a common locale for hauntings, populated by the dearly departed such as they were, but this tree in particular was a virtual hot spot, so to speak, for the restless dead. She couldn't help but wonder how many people had been strung from the cottonwood's limbs and left to die, kicking uselessly and struggling against the noose. Her stomach lurched, and she felt sick imagining the lives lost on this desecrated land.

The cuneiform symbols had been carved into the bark, high-up, and not very recently. The edges of the shapes were worn and rounded, but whatever magic it invoked was unbroken. Hannah imagined that in this tree's heartier years, its foliage would have easily hidden the carvings. Secrets were like that, though; given enough time, they became exposed.

Hannah held her Canon digital overhead, snapped a photo, and checked the display screen to see if she had gotten any of the carvings in-frame. The result was surprisingly good, and she smiled. Although it was broad daylight, she used the camera's built-in flash to eliminate the shadows of the branches, and the symbols stood out in stark relief. She took a few more photos, hoping to improve her luck a bit, rotating the zoom on the lens to get a closer shot. Satisfied, she let the camera hang from her neck and walked around the tree, studying the trunk for additional markings. She couldn't find any, which was for the best.

What she had seen already disturbed her enough.

***

Harlan Reynolds's mother was in her late forties but looked much older. Her wrinkles were more like deep caverns and her hair had bypassed premature graying and ran straight to shockingly white.

Mathilda had cracked the door just enough to peer out and stood silently waiting for Hannah to speak first. The younger woman introduced herself and held out a business card, which Mathilda read with equal silence, taking a moment to digest the admittedly obscure information printed upon it.

"Dr. Ford. A symbologist, hmm? With the University of Michigan? And on my doorstep why?"

"I'm here because of your son, Ms. Reynolds, and the rather unique symbols that were carved into the tree where he was found. First of all, though, let me express my deepest condolences. I'm so sorry for what was done to--"

The door closed in Hannah's face, her next words caught in her throat, stillborn. After a moment, though, as she was ready to turn around and leave, she heard a rattling of chains from inside the house and the door reopened.

If it were possible, Mathilda looked even older than she had only seconds before, and deflated. She stepped back as the door opened wider and she nodded her permission for Hannah to enter.

The small house stank of cigarette smoke, and Hannah noticed a number of discarded beer bottles near a worn recliner. Mathilda settled into the chair and adjusted the billowy mumu around her large legs.

"Thank you for your kindness about Harlan," Mathilda said. "I'm sorry I cut you off there. This is all rather much of a shock, you understand."

"I do, and I know this is unusual." Hannah opened her bag and fished around for the photos she had printed at a drugstore on her way to Seneca. "I won't take up much of your time, but I thought you would want to know I was looking into this. By any chance do you recognize these symbols?"

Mathilda stretched forward to receive the photos and peered at them closely. Her cheeks puffed out as she let out a long breath of air. "Do you know what they are?" Mathilda said.

Hannah nodded. "Yes, I do. What I don't know, or more accurately what I don't understand, is their relationship to Centralia and why there were cut into that tree."

"They not just in that tree, honey. They all over that town, you look close enough."

Hannah felt like she'd just been punched, and the news left her reeling. "Why?"

"To keep us out. And, when they can, to kill us."

***

"Centralia was a sundown town. You know what that was?" Mathilda said.

They had taken their conversation, and mason jars of iced tea, to the porch, needing some sunlight to shine over their dark conversations. Hannah sympathized, knowing it wasn't easy to sit alone for long in a home left suddenly empty by death. Sometimes you needed the light.

Hannah nodded, having learned this much about Centralia in her cursory research into the tiny community. A sundown town had laws prohibiting Blacks from being within its borders after sunset and prohibited their living there. It had been, for much of Centralia's existence, a legal method of segregation designed to protect the sensibilities and fears of its all-white citizens toward The Other, giving them a nice warm racist blanket to keep them safe and coddled.

"Saw pictures my grandma had," Mathilda said, "from back in the day. 'No

Blacks Allowed.' 'For White People Only.' That kinda shit. She even had her Green Book, still, and I said, 'Grandma, what's this book?'"

Hannah sat quietly, sipping on her tea as Mathilda spoke. She knew of Green Books, or, as they were published in the 1930s to the late 1960s during the height of America's segregation and the proliferation of sundown towns throughout the country, *The Negro Motorist Green Book*. The book was a resource to warn Black motorists about sundown towns and segregated areas where Black lives didn't matter a single bit.

Mathilda shook her head. "She told me about this book, how the places listed in it were places where Black people just up and disappeared, never to be seen or heard from again. I was born just a few years after the Jim Crow laws were killed, and grandma, she'd kept all that stuff as a reminder, and as a warning, too. Told me they may have taken the laws off the books, but they'd still find ways to kill us, grind us all down into the dirt. Grandma was right about that, weren't she?"

Mathilda took a healthy sip of tea, her throat clicking as she swallowed.

"Anyway. Centralia. Back in 1901, Grandma was just a little bitty slip of a thing, too young to remember what happened, but she liked her history, you know? She knew she'd been just a little baby, so she'd asked her momma and daddy about what happened in 1901 and they told her, and she told me. And now I'm gonna tell you, because you got to know. I told Harlan all about this town, its history, but, fuck, what did I know, right? I'm just his mom. Kids're like that, I suppose. I'm sure I was. Anyway. 1901."

Mathila wiped at the tears standing in her eyes and took another drink.

"Back then, if you were Black, you couldn't live in Centralia. A man named Whitmire tried to make a go of it, though, and when the whites found out about it they shot up his house, drove him and his family out of it, and burned the place down. Whitmire and his family, they had to flee out into the night with only the clothes on their back before they burned or got shot. Well, Whitmire returned," Mathilda said, a small smirk crossing her lips, "and he brought some friends with him.

"They shot the fuck outta that town," she said, laughing now. "Drove all them white folk back inside, made them taste a bit of that fear they tried to pay off on Whitmire. Papers back then had stories about it, 'Negroes Hold A Town,' course it was all shaded, you know, because being Black was a crime back then, and the whites were being unfairly targeted by this mob of angry Black folk they'd just tried to kill. Crazy innit?

"But Centralia was a sundown town, and in some of those sundown towns, Black people had a way of disappearing. Just, poof, gone. Never to be seen or heard from again."

Hannah thought of the symbols on Centralia Cemetery's big, old cottonwood tree, how they had looked aged and weathered, a part of that tree for a very, very long time. She wasn't an arborist or an archeologist, but she didn't think that carving could have been more than a century old. But she did suspect that it had been re-carved, the scarring made deeper, fresher, over the course of the last 120 years.

"Grandma didn't know what all happened exactly, because her parents didn't know either. All they had was rumors and guesses. But those Black people that went into Centralia with Whitmire, not a single one of them ever came back out. Not one of them. Nobody knows what happened, and eventually Black people learned that if they valued their life, they stayed the fuck out of Centralia.

"Now and again, you get some cocksure young fool, thinks he's all that, gonna try and mess with things, thinks just because there ain't no sundown laws on paper no more that it's all oh so copacetic, he can do what he wants. Centralia, that town reminds us it ain't so. It makes examples out of them such folks, gives us public reminders of how we need to mind our Ps and Qs, know our place. And Harlan…my boy…he just the latest in a long, long line of reminders going back to the day that fucking town was founded.

"That town is evil, Dr. Ford. Its people is evil. I was younger, I mighta said that town was cursed, but it ain't cursed for *them*, and it's a curse they made. We the ones that're cursed."

Hannah leaned forward in her chair slightly, her elbows resting on her knees. "Do you know what these symbols mean, Mathilda?"

"I don't, not exactly. Neither did grandma. She just said they was bad juju, and I can't say I disagree none."

Calling the carvings in that tree *bad juju* was an understatement, and Hannah debated how much to share with Mathilda. She was used to being met with skepticism by many, even those who had deliberately sought her help or advice regarding abnatural occurrences, like various officials in law enforcement at both federal and local levels. But Mathilda had a right to know, she decided. The woman's only child had been brutally murdered. And given some of what Mathilda had just shared with her, and, more importantly, those things she had left unsaid, Hannah suspected the woman would be open to what she had to say.

"Well, they are definitely bad," Hannah said. She took a deep breath, stalling just a bit to collect her thoughts and brace herself.

"And you're right, they are a curse on outsiders, or at least those that were defined as outsiders by whoever made these carvings. Are you at all familiar with a group of people called Thule?"

"Uh uh," Mathilda said, shaking her head.

"Over the course of human history, there have been various cultures, groups, and organizations identifying themselves as Thule. To the ancient Greeks, Thule was a place that existed beyond the borders of the known world. Nazi occultists believed Thule was also a place, one they called Hyperborea, and that it was where the Aryan race originated.

"The symbols carved into the tree where your son was found, they're a language. They're Hyperborean."

"You saying Nazis killed my boy?"

Hannah shifted uncomfortably in her lawn chair. "Not precisely, although I'm not ruling it out. Thule cults have existed in a variety of forms for a very, very long time, and although the Thule Society and the Nazi Party were closely aligned due to common, shared beliefs regarding white supremacy, not all Nazis were Thule, and not all Thule were Nazis. Thule obviously predates the Nazis, and has survived quite well on its own following World War II. And the words etched into this tree are most certainly a Thule language."

"What do they say?"

"I can't speak to specifics -- I'm not well-versed in Hyperborean -- but they point to a sacrifice being made to feed their gods."

Mathilda's mouth opened, then closed. She looked ready to say something, but at a loss for words, she drank from her jar. After the quiet stretched on for a time, a tear falling down her deeply lined face, she said, "What're we gonna do about it?"

The question had been on Hannah's mind since she'd first seen the pictures online, and it had only grown more persistent after she had verified the veracity of those photos with her own eyes.

"You got a ladder I can borrow?" Hannah said.

***

Returning to the cemetery during the day was too risky. Hannah didn't know if any services were scheduled, but she imagined the graves would have visitors or groundskeepers tidying up, or fresh holes being dug for future burials. The day brought too many unknown elements that could hinder her ability to break the spell cast upon that tree by those runes. The night brought its own share of risks given Centralia's enforcement of their still lingering, but unofficial sundown rules. She could still hear the sheriff warning her off the town, telling her about how skittish people got after sundown when it came to non-whites.

She spent much of the morning with Mathilda, although they spoke little. The grieving woman showed her pictures of Harlan, from the time he was a chubby little baby right on up to his high school senior photos. He'd been an athlete during his school years, playing baseball and basketball. Hannah watched the years melt with each turn of the page, and Harlan shed the baby fat as his tiny boy's body became that of a man's. And then they hit the end of the photo album and there were only a handful of blank pages left in the book.

Eventually, Hannah excused herself, telling Mathilda she had things to prepare and that she would return later for the ladder. She hadn't lied but had still felt guilty leaving this woman alone with her broken soul and the pain of memories. The quiet had gotten to her, had grown too thick and uncomfortable, and she couldn't figure out a way through it.

She spent several hours driving the streets of Centralia, trying to spot the Hyperborean runes that Mathilda claimed the small town was rife with. They hadn't been easy to find, but she did manage to spy several artifacts hiding in plain sight. The cuneiform symbols had been used as decorative flourishes for the door and window mouldings around City Hall. There were additional decorative runes on the plaques of statues, or over the entrances of local shops. By themselves, the carvings had few magical properties, acting more like an amplifier or reinforcement for the Hyperborean magic carved into the cemetery's cottonwood. That tree was the focal point, a sort of antenna, for the magic.

Turning to her computer, she spent a few hours engaged in research. After some deep web work, she was able to link the cuneiform runes to certain spells mentioned in the *Oera Linda*, an ancient occult manuscript from antiquity that had been rediscovered in the 1860s and was eventually dubbed "Himmler's Bible" due to the Nazi officer's obsession with the tome. Himmler so fully believed in the ancient writings from *Oera Linda* that he founded the Ahnenerbe, a think tank that primarily concerned itself with utilizing the occult to fulfill Hitler's goals of achieving racial purity. Between the mid-1930s and mid-1940s, the Ahnenerbe had conducted a number of expeditions across Europe, Africa, the Arctic and Antarctic to trace the influence of Hyperborean legacies on Earth, and record pagan and witchcraft rituals in an effort to summon their Thule gods and divine the future.

The links to Nazi occultism likely weren't relevant at all, but they did provide her with a path toward understanding Thule society and their beliefs. If what Mathilda's grandmother had said about Blacks disappearing in 1901 was any indication, then Thule activity in Kansas predated World War II by several decades. As a researcher and academic, though, she knew that in order to understand what happened in the past, you sometimes had to look at what followed and examine subsequent events.

Thule occultists existed long before the rise of Adolf Hitler, and the Nazis had merely popularized and adopted those ancient beliefs for their own diabolical ends. They were ancillary to what had happened in Centralia in 1901 and were occurring still to this day. America was a country of immigrants, and those people brought with them their own cultures and beliefs. It wasn't much of a leap to recognize that somebody along the way had brought their Thule customs to the shores of the US, and that they had, eventually, settled in Centralia and weaponized their racist ideology. Although the timeline of events made it clear that person or group of people couldn't have been Nazis, it was the Nazi's obsession with Thule occultism and lore in the decades that followed that allowed Hannah to gain a deeper insight into that fringe legacy. If it weren't for the horrors of World War II, she might not have recognized the 1901 carvings for what they were.

Sometimes you had to go forward to go back.

Harlan Reynolds had been sacrificed. Hannah had told Mathilda that much, but she had not told the boy's mother the full truth. His body had been sacrificed, but his soul was still bound to this realm as an offer in waiting to a destroyer god the Oera Linda referred as "The Masked God." Hannah could only imagine the torment the boy must be experiencing in such confinement, trapped and unable to pass, and she hoped that by breaking the curse that bound him he would be able to move on to whatever peace awaited him in the afterlife.

She felt a fresh surge of anger toward the men that had lynched Harlan. It hadn't been enough to kill him. They'd denied him a long life and a peaceful death and continued their torment of him even after his physical self had been extinguished. They had tortured him, and they kept on torturing him, even as he moved beyond this realm and into the next. She curled her fists at the injustice, the atrocity of it all, and wanted to slam her hands down upon the computer, to break it and fling its pieces across the room. Instead, she forced herself to breathe, forced herself to relax. There was nothing that could have been done for Harlan in life, but she had a chance to help him in death, and she would do everything she could for him.

By the time she finished her research and stood, her body stiff from having sat for too long, she noted the sun was setting.

***

The cemetery was empty after midnight, but Hannah kept her lights off as she drove down the marked path between the tombstones. Centralia Cemetery wasn't gated, which struck her as odd, if not downright archaic, having grown up in the city. It was just a simple plot of land defined by Cemetery Road and the trails that looped around the graves.

After only a few minutes, she was back at the too-familiar cottonwood. In the golden light of the full moon above, the ancient, gnarled trunk and its thick limbs reaching toward the heavens looked downright sinister. Mathilda's breath caught in her throat as she took in the sight. This tree was one of the last things Harlan would have seen.

"You ready?" Hannah said.

"Yeah."

Hannah squeezed Mathilda's thigh, and the older woman put her hand on Hannah's to squeeze her back. Mathilda offered a weak smile, one that wasn't strong enough to reach her eyes.

"Let's get that ladder, then," Hannah said.

As she unfolded herself from the driver's seat, Hannah put her bag over her shoulder, reassured by the weight of its contents. She tapped the leather, cool from the Jeep's air conditioner, and felt the outline of the Sig Sauer pistol that she carried as a general precaution. Satisfied that she was as prepared as she could be, she opened the back hatch and began pulling the ladder out. It was a long piece of equipment and they'd had to stand it on its side and work it between the driver and passenger seats, so Mathilda helped guide it from the front and made sure it didn't snag and tear up the interior.

Hannah unfolded and extended the ladder and set it up against the trunk of the tree, the top step coming to rest just beneath the sigil. She was careful of the surrounding branches as she climbed, not wanting to get poked in the eye or have her face scratched up. She couldn't help but notice the broken branches from where Harlan had unwillingly, painfully, and violently ascended this same tree. The mental imagery was disturbing, but her mind ran through the ugly scenario despite it, and she could all too easily imagine the noose being tossed around the tree's thickest upper limb, the white men below pulling on the other end, or using one of their cars to haul the rope, as Harlan's body rose, hands uselessly trying to pry loose the coils of rope from around his neck, legs kicking at the air. His flailing body would have snapped the younger, thinner branches on the way up as he struggled against his approaching end.

The temperature plummeted, her breath fogging the air. She took a quick look down at Mathilda, who seemed untroubled. Likely, the poor woman hadn't noticed the change at all. Hannah knew she was more sensitive than most to the abnatural, and spirits recognized and responded to this. In a way, she was a conduit for them to make themselves known. Others, like Mathilda, would go their entire life never suspecting the presences that surrounded them. But Hannah, spoke for them when she could and helped them move on if possible. So she climbed, not daring to look down again.

She came eye-level with the Hyperboran writing and could feel the electric charge of the magic, the hair on the back of her arms and neck standing on end. She swallowed, her mouth dry and heart hammering, and reached into the purse, her hand sweaty despite the chill only she felt. Her fingers coiled around the knife handle and --

The roar of engine noise broke through the midnight silence, followed by the grinding of tires rushing to a stop on dirt roads, rocks plinking against metal and earth.

Hannah risked a look over her shoulder, needing to work fast. The sheriff's car was in the lead and Morell was the first one out, hand going directly to the pistol on his Sam Browne belt. She couldn't see Mathilda below her, but she knew the gun was aimed right at Harlan's mother.

She freed the knife from her bag, her arm rising with it just as the ladder shook. She tumbled sideways, her hands snatching at the air for something to hold onto, and then she was falling. Pointy fingers snatched at her face, and warm blood spilled across her cold skin. The air came out of her in a pained gasp when she hit the ground, a flash of lightning shooting through her jolted spine and hips. The back of her head cracked painfully off the ground, rattling her brain. It took her a moment to breathe again, and in that time a lean white face filled her vision. She recognized him from the other day at the diner. Sheriff Morell. Recognition flashed in his eyes, too.

"Y'all never can listen and do what you're told, can you? I told you to stay out of this town come sundown, but here you are." Morell shook his head. "I ain't surprised, though. Fact is, I was counting on it, you see. I bet if I'd told you to look both ways 'fore crossing the street you'd just barrel head-down straight into rush hour traffic, wouldn't ya? That's how you people are, all of ya. Never listen, no respect. And now we gotta do this the old-fashioned way."

Hannah watched the frozen plumes of her breath break in the air as she gasped and struggled to roll over. The fall had fucked with her back and every movement was a fresh surge of agony. Hell, even breathing hurt.

Morell watched her struggle with a wry smile, then reared one leg back and kicked her hard, right in the ribs. Not hard enough to break bone, but she instantly knew that breathing wouldn't get any easier for her.

Mathilda was down on her knees, hands raised in the air over her head. Lying in the dirt, Hannah saw five others forming a half-circle around them, guns drawn. The headlights of the sheriff vehicles they'd arrived in had all been doused, but the moonlight provided enough to see by. She could see their goofy grins, the excitation plain on their faces as they gawped at their fresh catches for the night. The current of violence was strong in the air, and she knew, just knew, that everything was going to tilt sideways soon. She knew, with that self-same conviction, that she was looking at the lynch mob that had killed Harlan and had claimed the lives of many of the other restless spirits that lingered here and were bound to this massive, scarred cottonwood.

Morell stepped around her, holstering his service weapon, then knelt with his knee pressed into her aching spine. She grunted as rough hands pulled her arms behind her back, looping a plastic zip tie around one wrist, then the other. He continued to kneel on her, his weight pushing her down on the unyielding ground. He was suffocating her with his weight, and her entire torso protested in pain.

"Get off," she gasped.

Morell shifted slightly, putting even more of his weight on her and screwed his knee harder into her back. "Jenkens, you cuff that big one. I want both of these ready to go. Rest of you get your stuff together and get us prepped."

Hannah struggled to inhale, and each breath made her ribs ache. Morell kept her pinned to the earth until Jenkens was finished and Mathilda was left lying in the dirt on her stomach, her helpless eyes boring into Hannah's.

"I'm sorry," Hannah mouthed. Mathilda shut her eyes and seemed to nod before she was hauled to her feet.

Morell stood, then grabbed ahold of Hannah's biceps and hauled her to her feet. "Move," he grunted, pushing her into a walk as he led her to the patrol car. Hannah was shoved into the back of his patrol car while Mathilda was deposited in another.

She watched as the men moved between their vehicles, opening and closing the trunks, removing items that they carried over to the tree. Hannah had lost her folding knife in the fall, and her bag was in the grass near where she'd fallen, but she didn't consider herself helpless or the situation hopeless.

Hannah rotated her wrists in the too-tight zip ties, her hands already feeling numb from the loss of circulation. In a way, it was good Morell had squeezed the plastic loops around her as securely as he did. It made cutting herself easier, but the job was still time consuming. She just hoped there would be enough time to prepare.

As she worked her skin raw, she kept an eye on the policeman as they went from their cars to the tree. A large noose had been tossed over one of the tree's upper branches and candles had been arranged in a wide circle and lit beneath it. The men pulled on dark robes, the hoods obscuring their faces, and they knelt in prayer, hands joined. Hannah couldn't make out what they were saying, but she doubted it mattered. She'd seen sacrificial rituals before and while the gods and entities the practitioners worshipped varied, they all seemed to follow a similar process. The men were just getting warmed up, hyping themselves up for what was to come and working to shift their mental processes away from their jobs as police officers and into a more reverential mindset.

Warm blood slicked the plastic around her wrists, pooling between the zip ties and her skin. She continued working her hands back and forth, letting the plastic bite her deeper. She winced against the pain, compartmentalizing it as little more than a nuisance and gritted her teeth against it, the better to ignore it. The blood slick was growing thicker, her wrists turning more easily with the lubricant, and her palms grew wet.

Hannah dipped a finger against the opposite palm, as she shifted her butt closer to the edge of the hard plastic seat. There wasn't a lot of room to work with here, but it would have to do. With her wet finger, she began to draw on the seat behind her, leaving a trail of bloody shapes and signs built from memory. As she drew, she spoke in a dead language.

The car door opening interrupted her before the spell could be completed and Morell was grabbing her by the arm, hauling her out of the vehicle. He'd heard some of what she'd spoken and saw the mess she'd made of his seat.

"What the hell are you doing?" he asked, getting in her face so that they were chest to chest.

She said nothing and just let him fume. His face was hidden in shadows beneath the robe's hood, but she imagined he was red-faced and angry. She couldn't help but smile.

Morell slapped her across the face, then shoved her ahead of him, pointing her toward the tree. Jenkins came with Mathilda and the two women were led in a procession toward the noose that was awaiting them.

Hannah stared into Morell's eyes as he fitted the loop of rope around her neck. He was intent on securing the noose and she hoped her shoulders didn't move enough to signal she was drawing again, this time on the back of her shirt.

Morell stepped back and nodded toward somebody that Hannah couldn't see from somewhere behind her.

An engine started and an electric whine cut through the air. It didn't take her long to realize the noise was that of a winch and the rope was being pulled taught over the thick branch. The rough hemp bit into her neck, squeezing tight against her windpipe, and she was yanked off her feet. She rose into the air, kicking uselessly, trying not to panic and failing. Hannah couldn't breathe, and the weight of her suspended body was pulling on her strained neck and aching lungs. The rope tightened over her carotid arteries and she felt like she was slowly drowning. Her legs flailed, the primal part of her terrorized and seeking solid ground to stand on, and she had to fight against the fear to continue her bloody drawing. She just hoped the symbology was cogent enough and not too badly drawn to be useless. Blackness crept in around the edges of her vision and her mind swam. She tried to speak the words around a thickened tongue jutting between her lips, her eyes bulging and threatening to break free of their orbits.

A cold hand pressed against hers, and her first thought was Mathilda. But she knew that was wrong. Mathilda was still on the ground, and the hand was too immaterial. It was less a hand and more a suggestion of a hand, but it was comforting, nonetheless. She hated to pull away from it but had no choice. She had to keep drawing before she passed out.

Below, the men moved, but their actions were as indistinct as the words they were chanting. The language they spoke was guttural and ancient, but it had power. Hannah could feel the magic of their words as the air around her changed and grew hot. The hair on her arms rose in response to the building electric charge. It felt like the onset of a lightning storm.

She couldn't drag in enough air to speak, but she tried to gasp out the dead words as best she could, hoping it would be enough. The ephemeral hand squeezed hers, the cold fingers chilling her to the bone. Although the touch was deeply unpleasant, Hannah found a measure of reassurance in that touch. The hand grew stronger, if only briefly, and the plastic around her wrists snapped. Her hands felt heavy, as if they were filled with sand and needles. Dully, she reached overhead and grabbed onto the rope above her, trying to pull herself up just enough to relieve some of the pressure and let her breathe.

Lightning cut through the air, arcing through the branches of the tree. When Hannah had been little, her grandfather had bought her a ball lightning lamp, and she remembered staying up late to play with it, watching in awe as the electricity responded to her touch. Now, she felt like she was inside that lamp, hanging right in the middle of those arcing blasts of electricity and pulsing lights.

She was too weak to climb up the rope to the branch above, but what little movement she was capable of was enough to panic the men behind her. She couldn't hear the winch speed up, but she certainly felt it as her body shook in stops and starts as the rope was jolted lower and then back up again to repeat the process. They were trying to create enough of a drop to snap her neck or decapitate her.

Hands pressed against her, trying to help hold her up. She could only make out the faintest images of their beings, and there were more of them, this restless community of the dead, than she had suspected. While the little bit of magic she had worked wasn't strong enough to free them from the binding spell that held their souls in place, trapped within this tree, it had been enough to give them some degree of agency. She could feel their anger and pain as they swirled around her.

A streak of lightning danced too close, the heat of it burning a line across her shins. She needed to get down and away from this mess. Above, a loud cracking noise rose above the electric howl of the storm swirling around her and she was falling again. This time she was ready for it. What she wasn't ready for was what she saw as she fell.

High above the tree, the sky had broken apart and instead of stars she saw a strange and foreign land. The earth above was bleached white and built there were monochromatic structures that defied human geometry. Her brain ached to look at them, unable to process the imagery her optic nerves were transmitting. The shapes and lines made no sense, and she turned away from the portal, screaming, as she hit the ground.

The thick branch landed nearby. Chaos had erupted in the men, and some of the Sheriff's deputies were fighting with their robes to free their guns. Hannah knew she wasn't out of the woods yet, and she spied her knife and bag, dropped near the fallen ladder. She reached for the knife and unfolded it, and then was jerked back, the noose tightening again around her throat.

Her feet kicked for purchase in the soil as she was dragged backward. Somehow, she'd held onto the knife, but only barely. The handle was greasy with blood and mud. Rocks bit into her back and shoulders as the winch pulled her, and she reached overhead with the knife. Hannah sawed back and forth against the rope, struggling to breathe. Just as she began to lose hope, the rope snapped and she slid, painfully, to a stop, gasping for air.

Lying still for a moment, in the hopes that she could collect herself, get her racing heart under control, and fill her lungs, she grew aware of the fresh aches in her back. The rocks and hard earth she'd been dragged across had left her feeling skinned, and the back of her shirt was wet and sticky. She looked toward the tree but saw only lightning and the confusing sight of an alien realm. Whatever spirits were trapped by the Hyperborean magic were confined again. Her minor spell had been broken, but it had at least served its purpose. She was alive, and she had to get moving before she squandered that small opportunity.

Ignoring the catalog of aches and pains and bleeding wounds, Hannah forced herself to her feet. Small explosions marked each footfall as Morell and his deputies opened fire on her. Lucky for her, their aim was terrible. She tried to run, but after nearly being hanged and dragged to death her body was in too bad of shape. The best she could do was lurch and try to keep herself low, making as small a target of herself as her battered ribs allowed.

An awful noise broke over the sporadic gunfire and she couldn't help but look toward the sound. It came from above, high over the tree. She immediately wished she hadn't sought out the source of that noise, her mind reeling as her brain struggled to make sense of it all. The shapes of the buildings and, now, the creatures were too much of a confusing, jumbled mess. It wasn't just that she was looking at something so plainly alien and inhuman, but that her senses were trying -- and failing, badly -- to translate structures and lifeforms that existed and operated at a higher dimensional level than the three-dimensional space her brain inhabited and understood. The Hyperborean portal Morell and his men had opened was extra dimensional, a gateway to anti-de Sitter space.

And something was coming through it.

Suddenly, Hannah realized just how quiet the night had fallen. The sounds of gunfire had lapsed and even the electric hum of the portal's light show amidst the tree's branches was muted. Morell and his men stood gaping at the portal, watching as a massive, churning, bone-white blob of flesh pushed through. Witnessing this being's intrusion into three-dimensional space was supremely disorienting and Hannah's head ached trying to make sense of it. A throbbing pain pulsed behind her eyes and lit up the entire pathway of nerves deep into her brain. It felt like her mind was melting, and she wanted to drop to her knees, drive the blade of her knife into her throat and saw open the veins and arteries there and bleed out into the grass, welcoming the peace of oblivion and...

NO!

She shook her head, trying to rally her sanity amidst the insane. She heaved herself forward, toward her handbag and the ladder. She had to destroy the Hyperborean sigil and close the gateway before things got any worse.

Gunfire erupted into the night once more, and she ducked her head low. The shots weren't being aimed her way this time. She twisted her head to see what the sheriff and his men were doing, then wished she hadn't. They'd all lost their damn minds.

Jenkins had executed one of his fellow deputies and now stood watching the white blob breaching dimensions, his mouth agape and arms spread wide. Blood leaked from the orbits of his eyes like ruined mascara. As he shouted insensibly, he took his gun in both hands and shoved the barrel beneath his jaw, tight up against his throat. When he pulled the trigger, Hannah saw the back of his head come off.

"God!" she screamed, looking away too late.

She wiped blood out of her own eyes, felt more pooling in her ears, afraid to look at the seething tumor of flesh birthing its way through the portal above. Morell was screaming at his men, ordering them to stop firing, to put their guns down, but he was being ignored. His men were too afraid, their minds too far gone for rational thinking, and they were shooting in a craze-fueled panic.

The fleshy blob drooped lower and began to unfold, reaching toward Morell and his men. It hadn't even touched one of them when a man's tortured scream rose over the gunfire. Hannah's gorge rose and she dry heaved into the grass at what she saw. The cop's innards were pulled free of his body and splattered across the graves behind him, his hollowed-out skin flopping uselessly to the ground.

It didn't even touch him, her mind shouted, *it didn't even touch him*. Over and over as she stumbled forward.

Finally, she reached her handbag and freed the Sig Sauer from it, tucking the gun into the back of her waist. Then she was righting the ladder, a metallic clang ringing in the night as it smacked against the tree.

"Didn't even fucking touch him," she said, unable to believe it. She understood it, but she was goddamned if she could believe it. A few years ago, she had attended a theoretical physics seminar at her university about higher dimensional space. The group of panelists had spent some time discussing the possibilities of mankind existing in higher dimensions and what would happen if higher dimensional lifeforms inhabited three-dimensional space.

"Because a four-dimensional creature exists outside the boundaries of three-dimensional space, they would be able to see everything in our realm, the same way we can look down on a 2-D object and see everything. They would be able not only to see you, but to see *inside* you," the faculty member had said. Then, flashing a wicked smile, he added, "They'd be able to reach down inside you and pull out your organs without even breaking your skin!"

There were laughs at that, along with some gasps and squirms, and the faculty member had looked rather pleased with himself for his gross-out moment of the seminar. Hannah had laughed, too, thinking it was little more than bullshit theatrics from a young professor enjoying the limelight.

"Son of a bitch had been right," Hannah said, climbing the rungs as fast as she could. She occasionally looked back to see what was happening, worried that Morell or his depleting stock of cops might start shooting at her again. She turned away before she had to watch another one of the deputies kill himself, but not before she saw him kill another fellow officer. Morell's homicidal Thule cult was quickly devolving into suicidal sacrifices to their inchoate god. Clearly, this night had not gone as they had planned.

The hair all along Hannah's body stood on end, responding to the blanket of static electricity covering the air. Flashes of lightning danced all around her, but, blessedly, refused to make contact. It felt like when you tried to push matching ends of a pair of magnets together, her whole body thrumming in repulsion to the currents surrounding her. And her head – God, did it ever ache! Her brain felt like a throbbing, clenched fist, like it was ready to punch its way out of her skull.

Reaching the top of the thick cottonwood tree, she raised the knife and stabbed it into the gnarly bark, twisting the blade to break away pieces of the old, thickly lined skin. She hacked deeper, drawing new lines into the ancient sigil, corrupting its meaning, transforming it -- destroying it.

Lightning flashed and there was a massive crack as a tree limb snapped. The bushy head of the cottonwood went up with a *whoomph!* of flames, fire spreading across the dry limbs and leafy greens.

Hannah scrambled as best she could back down the ladder, the smoke already growing thick and making her cough. The summer had been dry in Kansas and the flames spread fast. By the time she reached the ground, fire was dancing all across the top of the tree, thick, black smoke billowing into the air, reaching toward the portal and the unfolding blob of flesh above.

A moment later, the portal was gone and the white flesh was falling. It landed in the flames, sparks and ash flying as it tumbled through the blazing vegetation that had become its funeral pyre. Hannah watched it burn, satisfied. And then she remembered Mathilda and Sheriff Morell.

The latter laid still in a pool of blood. He'd taken his own life, and the top of his head was a grisly, pulpy mess that her eyes refused to linger on.

"Mathilda!" she cried. Hannah couldn't find the woman, and she called for her again.

"Here!" Mathilda shouted back.

Hannah followed the older woman's voice, heading toward the police cruisers. Mathilda was struggling to rise above the back end of the Ford. Hands still bound, she'd run off and taken cover. Smart.

"Turn around," Hannah said. "Let me get those damn things off you."

She flicked the knife and the zip ties came off Mathilda's wrists with ease.

"My God," Mathilda said, watching the fire burn, an orange glow lighting up the cemetery and its field of fresh bodies.

Hannah led her back to the Wrangler, helping her inside. "I owe you a new ladder."

"Nah, don't worry about that." Mathilda looked like she wanted to say more, and Hannah waited, her eyes silently encouraging the woman to speak her mind. Finally, she did.

"I thought... I thought I saw Harlan there, under that tree. Saw him, and...

and felt him."

Hannah smiled, and the two women hugged, Mathilda softly crying into Hannah's shoulder.

"I did, too," Hannah said. "He's at peace now."

Mathilda cried freely, and in her tears she thanked Hannah Ford for that.

***

After the women said their goodbyes, Hannah returned to the motel for a few hours of sleep. She was looking at another long drive back to Michigan and needed rest before she hit the road again. Sleep wouldn't come, though. Lying with her head on the pillow, her mind kept racing and refused to slow down, until, finally, she pulled out her laptop and began writing a case report detailing the last two days in Centralia.

Her thoughts were a jumbled mess and it was a struggle to make sense of it all in an orderly, let alone coherent, fashion. She was still having difficulty processing all that she had seen only a few hours ago. She'd never seen a dimensional breach before, although she knew they had happened a number of times previously over the course of humanity's legacy. There had been plenty of small breaches conjured, and even a few on larger scales in places like New York and Arkham, Massachusetts, but those events had been more than two hundred years ago if she recalled correctly.

She recalled thinking that Morell and his men had been taken off-guard by this evening's (or was it this morning's?) occurrence, and they had certainly been susceptible to the mind-shattering nature of dimensional intrusions. She thought, too, of Mathilda's grandmother and her stories of the missing Black men and women that had violated Centralia's sundown laws, and the hanging of Harlan Reynolds. Hannah felt it was extremely likely those earlier disappearances were linked, that those poor people had been sacrificed and lost to another dimension, or else were killed and buried, never to be recovered.

Human sacrifice was risky business, and it didn't always capture the attention of the intended deities. Most often, mankind was simply ignored. Portals were opened and closed with little attention paid by the target audience on the other side. Lives were sacrificed with nary an eyebrow raised, and people like Morell got it into their heads to keep on trying until they got it right, likely unsure of what, exactly, they were trying to summon.

But the more they kept trying, the more dark psychic energy that was built up over time upon the altar of death -- in this case, the hanging tree at Centralia Cemetery -- the more likely this primitive human race was to finally be noticed, like the annoying fly circling the head of a greater creature, buzz buzz buzzing until they finally got swatted.

The more Hannah thought about it, the more confident she felt that this was exactly what had happened. Morell, and the generations that had preceded him, had killed as many Black folk as they could to honor their Thule gods, but whatever portals they had opened had gone unheeded by those in Hyperborea. Eventually, after 120 years of bloodshed, 120 years of Black lives lost to these white men's racist rituals, the Hyperboreans finally took notice.

Guess the Thule weren't impressed by all that so-called white superiority, she thought, a wry smile cracking her lips. She couldn't help but laugh, although she found none of it funny. It was either laugh or go crazy, and she'd already gone half-crazy once this evening. So, laugh it was.

When she finally got herself back under control, she wiped away a tear, her sides aching.

Hannah finished her briefing, gave it a read over and added some additional thoughts and clarifications as they came to her, then read through it a second time. Satisfied, she saved it to her hard drive, uploaded it to a cloud storage service, then emailed the report to her handler with herself CC'd as an additional backup.

She closed the lid and put the computer back in its carry-bag. Sunrise was only a few hours away and she was exhausted.

Sleep came easier now that her mind was unburdened, and she sank into a deep rest, her alarm set for early afternoon.

When she awoke, she loaded the Jeep, settled her bill, and drove, putting Centralia behind her forever.

Hannah vowed to never fucking return to fucking Kansas.

A Certain Kind of Forest Sound

Adam Cesare

Centralia, TX

Location of Centralia, Texas (unincorporated community in Trinity County)

Coordinates: 31°15′29″N 95°02′24″W

Country   United States

State   Texas

County   Trinity

Population

• Total   53

First Epicenter Sighting

• January 1983

Percent Burn

• 23%

When people talk about hiking and nature and shit, they say how they enjoy the quiet.

But it's not the quiet I like.

It's the noise.

Davy Crockett National Forest is full of noise, which is why I come here so often. I like to listen.

Like to see what my ears can pick out.

Of course, there are the easily identifiable sounds. Real newbie shit—birds chirping, leaves rustling, and the drip and babble of the creeks and tributaries that run along the trails.

But under and between those sounds there's the animal noises you only learn to identify once you've walked long enough, spotted enough tails and whiskers.

There's the 'eeee eee ee' sound of fox squirrels preserving the species. The frustrated smack of an otter, banging a freshwater mussel against a rock. The "best back the fuck up" sizzle of a rattlesnake.

Oh, you know what a rattler sounds like? Cute.

Sure, woodpeckers are easy enough to identify too. When they're close. But a mile or two distant and they're near indistinguishable from semi-automatic weapons fire. Of which there's more than woodpeckers, since guns aren't a protected species in Texas.

I'm always searching for new sounds, though, and more often than not when I go on these hikes: the woods provide.

You'll laugh, tell me I'm nuts, but I've learned to identify the sounds of several—what should I say? 'Cryptids' is too specialized a word, makes me sound like I'm some kind of scientist, which I'm not. I guess I prefer 'undiscovered creatures.' And I'm not just talking about the knocks and vocalizations of sasquatches, either. Which is your basic bitch woodland monster.

No, I've heard, and then seen with my own eyes, giant owls, big enough to prey on hog. Not Mothman, mind you, but bigger than a barn owl, that's for sure.

I have heard, tracked, and glimpsed what I'm assuming is what people have seen when they describe a wampus cat or Ozark Howler.

You find all kinds of shed antlers dotting the trails too. But don't think I'm saying those are from jackalope.

Jackalopes aren't real. But sometimes it does seem like more antlers than there can be deer. Odder shapes, too.

I think these things reveal themselves to me because they know I won't tell on them. They hear me coming like I can hear them. But something about the way I'm walking, or holding myself, or maybe it's that they smell me if I'm downwind… something about me doesn't scare them off.

That or these things I've seen, they're hallucinations and I'm undiagnosed crazy.

No way to tell, really. How would I know?

See, I spend most of my day inside.

I run a small business, located outside Lufkin, down 94 from here. You may have passed it. It used to be a karate studio. When it was my dad's. Well, he's dead and he never taught his daughter karate and I'm the only one of the siblings who wanted the building.

Probably for the best, because times change. I bought a new sign, salvaged what I could of the interior and now it's an MMA gym. Which is similar, but different enough.

I find that my daily routine—re-racking weights, mixing the Lysol solution we use to clean the mats, occasionally putting a teenage boy in an armbar— mean that I'm not eager to spend my free time at home.

I need fresh air.

So I drive the twenty-something minutes from the gym to where Davy Crockett's lush.

When I get here, I vary my approach. Walk a number of different routes. Sometimes those set for hiking and sometimes the narrow, unmarked deer paths.

But I mostly try to stay north.

Not because the woods are better. Not because it helps avoid the need to walk through private property, since, even though this whole area's considered the forest, there's homes and businesses in the areas to the south.

I stay north because I don't want to risk wandering into somewhere I don't want to be.

Namely Centralia.

But you probably guessed that.

Not that the Centralia in Texas really has borders. Not that it's much of a location at all.

And not that I'm superstitious.

Look, I come to the forest to *relax*. And, remember, I'm the gal finding Chupacabra scat. On a good day, under normal conditions, I attract weird.

So why do I need to be tempting fate by walking through an unincorporated, loosely accursed, township?

Today I've ranged close, though. Closer than I'd like.

And I'm getting even closer, as we speak.

It's because of that sound.

Hear it?

No, of course you cain't.

Can't.

Forgive me. When I get talking, I get folksy, I guess.

My dad used to be that way. Would tell stories in that 'come here let me spin you a yarn' style.

Always struck me as a put-on, inauthentic.

Then he'd turn around and make fun of the way *I* talked. How I tried to a-nun-see-ate and try not to sound like I'm from where we're from.

Used to say "Celia's got her TV voice on."

Well, it wasn't like *Celia* was practicing her katas with her brothers, was it?

Oh, yeah.

I was telling you about the sound.

How to describe it? It's like a… like a…

More like a *vibration* than anything else.

Which, yeah, no duh, that's what all sounds are, vibrations. But this is different. It's the height of a tuning fork's twang. That sound extended, looped and sustained.

I've been hiking for the better part of the afternoon—now approaching evening—and it still doesn't seem to be getting any louder. And no cleaner, either. It still has that slight warble inside, not sounding like any forest sound I've ever heard.

If I didn't know any better, I'd say the sound is mocking me. Staying just on the periphery of my knowing, my understanding.

At least it's summer, it gets dark later, won't be full night for another couple hours. Otherwise, I'd have to cut back to the road, try not to get hit as I worked my way back to my truck, using my phone's flashlight to watch where I'm stepping.

I haven't lost that much track of time. Or at least, I should say, haven't been lost following this damn thing for too long.

There. Hear it?

It's a hum, and I step, and it's still a hum, and I step but it doesn't get any louder.

But if I take a couple of steps backward?

It recedes.

Almost like it's issuing a threat that it *will* go away, and that I'll never be able to find it again unless I keep following it now. Tonight.

I reach a break in the woods. A field. Not mowed grass behind fenceposts, but still the sense that this land is kept. Owned. Before I step out of the tree-line, I look both ways to make sure I'm not going to stumble into someone sitting out on a lawn chair, a shotgun over their knees, couple empties at their feet.

No one out here. Nothing in this field either. Just tall grass and a couple of overachieving lightning bugs, sparking in the daylight.

The sound is telling me that the best way to find it is by walking straight across. Through this field, not around.

So I do.

And I make it about halfway, length of a football field, maybe two? I don't know. Can't judge these things. And the field's probably too many octagons wide to count, if I were to try and measure it in sports I understand, that I've been allowed to participate in.

As I'm stepping over that halfway mark, the sound finally changes.

I hear it in my left ear now and my left ear only.

Working my jaw up and down, like it's possible my ear's popped, I look around, then turn and take two steps to the left.

Yup. You get it now. This way. The sound is saying. It fills both ears after I hook that 90 degree turn to the left.

Look. I am keenly aware that whatever this sound is, it may mean to do me harm. That you, the audience member might be yelling up at the screen.

But I can take care of myself.

And that's not tough-gal bravado. Not posturing.

I'm stronger than most. Just a fact.

Those brothers with their katas?

Stronger than them. Broke Kasey's collarbone when I was 11 and he was 14. Not on purpose, but because I had to. *The Care Bears Movie* was on. Network premiere.

My dad? Kicked his ass once or twice, too. First time was toward the end of high school because he tried to do that macho 'don't touch my little girl shit' to my prom date. Date had already touched plenty.

Second time, I don't want to talk about that. Wasn't a fair fight. I was being stupid.

"Celia," you ask, "Didn't you say your dad is dead? You didn't…"

No. I wouldn't bury the lede like that. I didn't kill my dad. This isn't one of those stories where you find out the teller is some kind of irredeemable monster by the end.

At least I hope it's not.

Let's see how this mysterious sound thing goes.

I come to the edge of the clearing and enter another stand of trees, but the woods are nowhere near as dense as what I traverse regularly to the north of here.

No, if I squint I can see straight through to the other side. And that another field awaits me. The sound calls from beyond these trees, no louder but somehow closer, I'm sure of it. I answer the call by stepping over logs, my boots sucking deep in mud that didn't seem to be an impediment earlier in my walk.

A fox squirrel chitters at me from somewhere above. I'm in his territory.

Or this is one of the squirrels that knows me and he's asking me why I'm out so late. Why I'm so far south. Why I've crossed over into Centralia territory.

I don't have a good answer for him.

Before I'm into the next field, I notice a new sound. It's not *the* sound, but it's close to it.

Bees.

Where the last clearing had lightning bugs, this one's got bees.

A shitload of them.

I step out, intrigued and distracted enough that I don't look both ways like I did last time. Don't check to see that I'm alone out here, even though I should check because I'm definitely on someone's property.

To keep following the sound I need to dip under a fence.

As I stride toward the center of the clearing, the bees hover around me. It's like I'm being given a bee police escort. Dozens of them encircle my arms, make lazy waves in between my legs, tickle the span of my shoulders with their wings. Which is quite a span: I can lift more than you. It's the trade-off for meal prep that solely consists of freezer bags full of tasteless, boiled chicken breasts.

I'm not worried about the bees stinging me. Dusted yellow from a day's work, they don't seem like the stinging type.

I look ahead to my destination.

Peeking out from behind a copse of trees at the base of this clearing is a house. The whitewash is grey, brown, and green with age and weather, but the house itself too obscured by the trees to tell if it's abandoned or just generally janky.

But I'm not walking to the house.

The sound isn't coming from the house.

There's another structure out here.

The boxes are much smaller than the house, but they command all of my attention. Six white wood boxes, four stacked two high and the other two freestanding, on the sides. The white of the boxes isn't stained and old like the whitewash of the house. Paint's fresh, seems to glow in the early evening.

Huh. I look up at the sky. Early evening, turning to later evening fast. Seems like I *may* be walking home in the dark. Never was good at time management.

But that doesn't matter.

Because this is it.

The hairs on my body are pins, even the downiest of my lady hairs. Too much information?

These six boxes arrayed in front of me is where the sound's coming from.

And now it is different, because it's not only the specific sound that's been calling to me for miles, but layered on top of that is the orchestra of different bee sounds that feed into the functioning of a hive. Bees landing, taking off, eating, shitting, spewing up wax and honey and tending to their squirming larva, their future foot soldiers. I can hear that all and more, in addition to the sound.

These boxes are, taken as a whole, a—the word for it eludes me right now.

They're beehives. The kind tended for their honey. Kept just the right temperature so that the queens at the center of each box can do their job, command their colony.

Fuck. What're they called?

Ah, thanks.

Apiary.

I'm standing in front of an apiary. And underneath these bee boxes, like an underground river or a swirling ball of energy, pulses the sound.

I've got to get closer to it.

But whoever's built this apiary has fenced it in with a double layer of chicken wire. And on top of the wire mesh is a single thick metal cable that I trace back to a car battery.

Is it really electrified or are they just bluffing?

Probably not bluffing. Since there are plenty of black bear around here who, if cartoons are to be believed, love honey.

But I've got slightly more sense than a bear, so I begin to undo the plastic nuts on the battery, denature the sizzling metal cable.

While I'm working, the sound begins to talk to me. Not inside my ears, necessarily. Feels deeper than that. Like it's hooked up directly to where my spine meets my brain stem.

And it's not speaking to me in English. Not in any language I can put mouth sounds to at all. As hard to parse as this ineffable feeling is, I know for sure that it is a kind of communication.

Listening slows my work, causes me to snag my thumb on a jagged end of chicken wire as I pull away the first layer, intent on getting to the boxes, getting closer to the sound.

Hard to tell what the sound's trying to describe to me in the unlanguage it beams directly into my grey matter, but maybe if I get closer, get inside the boxes of the apiary, I'll be better able to understand.

I catch the odd snippet of an idea though. I am presented with concepts that I can almost grasp. But I can't tell if the sound is saying 'evil' with a little e or evil with a big E.

Whether the apocalypse that it's suggesting to me, the one I'm seeing in the space of brain between my ears is a *personal* apocalypse or a *global* one.

And before I can breach the beehives' final line of defense, the last flimsy layer of chicken wire, before I can get the answers I both need and dread, I hear something else.

"Can we help you?"

The words break the sound's spell over me so fast that the cold-water shock of being back on earth, not zonked out in honey bee space, makes me nauseous.

"Ma'am. He's talking to you."

Uh. Ma'am?

I turn slow, thinking about what I said earlier about there being more guns than woodpeckers out here.

Woodpeckers. Peckers. Peckerwoods.

My stomach evens out as I complete my turn, exhale and take stock of the situation that's approached from behind while I was distracted.

The *three* situations. Each standing only a few strides from me.

They're armed, but not NRA armed. Which is some kind of silver-lining.

The big one—I think the one who called me 'Ma'am'—is holding a baseball bat.

The little one, the one who spoke first, holds himself like a natural leader, isn't holding anything but a phone.

But it's the girl—the female of the pasty species—that I instantly clock as the most dangerous. She's got a kitchen knife, pearl knuckles, and her hands are shaking.

A father, a brother, and a sister?

Are they all siblings, the little one not the father, just an older brother who's drank himself a big papa belly?

Doesn't matter. Knowing how these three are related wouldn't really help me now anyway.

I wonder if they can hear the sound. If they can, maybe they've gotten used to it.

"There's nothing for you in there," the little one says, motioning toward the hives with his empty hand. "Get. I've already called the cops."

A bee alights on my right earlobe. I can hear its buzz like a vacuum cleaner. But I don't swat. If I move too fast, they'll be on me.

Or at least Missy will. The other two, hard to tell.

"Look at her, Eric. You think she's a junkie or something?" the girl asks.

"Kind of jacked for a junkie," the big one answers. I almost nod at the compliment. He may be the muscle, but he's not the dumb one.

In fact, I've clocked them as peckerwoods, but maybe that was unkind. Or at the very least, unfair. There's an intelligence behind all of their eyes, now that I'm looking, a canniness belied by how they're dressed.

Cigarette burnt tank top on the little one. Rolled sleeve work shirt on the big guy. Yellowed, floral pattern dress on Miss Stabsalot 1994.

"What's in them?" I hear myself ask before I think through whether I should.

The little one glances at his phone before answering, does it in a way that tells me he hasn't really called the cops, but that he's weighing his options.

"Um. Bees?"

"What's making that sound then?"

Shit. Again, I'm so scattered that I'm playing my cards before even looking at them. Hell, without even considering whether this is poker, gin, or Go Fish we're playing.

"She *knows*, Eric," the girl says, impatient. Her voice is needling Eric. Like she's saying, *You see, Eric? I told you we should have shot her from the porch.*

Like I said, I'm a good listener. I pick up on the nuances of sounds.

Well. I move my eyes between them all. End on the girl. Try and come to terms with the situation, even though it's still unclear what these three have stashed in the apiary.

The one thing I know is that they'll kill me to protect it.

I sigh. No use crying over it now. The die had been cast before any one of the four of us had spoken a word to each other.

"You didn't call the cops because the cops can't know whatever's in there with the bees. That about right, Eric?" I say.

The girl moves first. She's likely the fastest of the three, but doesn't realize—can't know—that when I teach self-defense classes at the rec center, we use a dummy blade about the size of her real one.

Like my size, like my strength, when I speak to the speed and fluidity of my fundamentals: it ain't bragging. It's just facts.

I take the knife away from her and run it across the back of Eric's hand before my trip can send her to the dirt.

He yelps, drops the phone, which is good. The phone's not a weapon, of course, but if we were to count it, then two of my three attackers are already disarmed.

The big guy grunts. Which isn't something you need to do, winding up with a baseball bat, only telegraphs your intentions, but guys that big seem incapable of resisting the grunt-urge.

I duck into a squat, and at the same time slide the knife into the meat of Eric's right thigh.

Poor guy. He's getting the brunt of it.

The tall guy doesn't follow through with his swing, can't because he'd hit Eric, so instead he pump-fakes, choking up on the bat and calling me a bad word as he menaces me with the weapon.

Eric tries to knee me with his good leg, but I'm already halfway to standing and his knee sails past the side of my head.

When the girl pounces, she doesn't growl, doesn't tell me what she's about to do like her brothers—brothers?—did, so I don't hear her pushing off gravel, launching herself at me until it's too late.

She manages to send me falling forward with her momentum, not her weight, because she can't be more than a hundred-twenty pounds.

I taste dirt as I fall flat, then feel her begin clawing my back.

Which is fine. Superficial wounds, at best. And what she's done is put me within grabbing distance of the car battery they'd used to rig their security system for the apiary.

I need both hands but it's light enough I can swing it around, turning from belly to side.

Under the corner of the magnet, I feel her teeth break inward in a way that makes me flinch. A sound and sensation like that is nails on a chalkboard, even if you're not the one being hurt.

I've broken plenty of other people's bones. Mostly I'm fine with it. But teeth and eye-stuff I can't stand. It grosses me out.

My follow-through gives the girl a jaw like a snake and she yowls so loud it drowns out the bees.

The bees but not the sound.

"You're dead," Eric yells at me, but it's not like he's jumping to help his sister/daughter. He's standing above us with both hands clamped, applying pressure to the wound in his leg meat.

I drop the battery, roll toward the other two combatants. A good third of a fight is assessing where you are in relation to the other guy. If I were to get to my feet where I am, it's not like the girl would be a problem, but Eric and the tall guy could get lucky and I could trip over a bee box or get snagged on chicken wire.

I'm in swinging distance and the tall guy might not be dumb, but he *is* impatient.

A big overhead swing pulverizes the dirt beside my head.

I rise and he chokes up even further, flicks his wrists, and catches me in the gut with the knob.

Even without much leverage, he winds me.

Fuck.

If he lands a blow to my head with one of those King Kong swings, I'm dead.

Can't let that happen, gotta end this quick.

I stretch out and borrow the knife from Eric.

It comes free with a straight line of blood and a zipper-whick sound.

At my full height I'm still only up to big boy's shoulders, which is perfect.

He grunts—his final mistake with all his family breathing—and I calmly step out of the way of his next swing.

He connects, making Eric's nose an innie.

While he's dismaying about what he's done, fratricide or patricide or whatever, I put the knife in his temple.

The girl hasn't been screaming through all of this, likely won't recover to what I've done to her face, but I go over to where she's laying and put boots to her like her hair's caught fire.

When it's over I cry.

More of an adrenaline thing than it is an emotional response.

Probably.

Look. I didn't lie to you. I said I didn't kill *my dad*.

I said nothing about sundry other assholes I've met along the way in life.

I hear something, for a half second think I've been discovered, that there's more of them, but when I look back at the tree line I see that there's a forest creature watching me.

Could be a bear, could be something else. Hard to tell in the quickening dusk.

The maybe-bear regards me for a moment, watches the big woman crying over three dead bodies, and then goes about its business.

When I manage to count to ten between involuntary sobs, I wipe my eyes and allow my attention to turn back to the sound.

The sound has faded now. Almost like these three jokers being alive fed it somehow, made it stronger, gave it its hold over me.

Not sure what I expect to find, I begin prying open the lids to the bee boxes.

What I see makes a certain sense, but is still something that'll weigh on me, something that, in a few months or years that I might look back on and say 'yup, that was the start of it.' A revelation that might well end with my violent death.

The bees sting and sting as I excavate. I'm not allergic, so their sacrifice for queen and colony means nothing to me. I think I can hear tiny screams as their stingers pull lose from their bodies, but maybe that detail's in my imagination.

I stop feeling the stings by the time I'm opening up the third box. And I don't bother with the fourth, fifth or sixth, because what's it going to change?

Inside each box in the apiary there's a severed head.

Of course, there's honeycomb and bees and larva too.

But the thing you notice first is the severed head.

The head in the first box is the freshest. A bee wiggles out of one nostril, the eyes frosted over with slight decomposition, the neck severed with a hacksaw or something similar.

The second head's a little worse.

And the head in the third box is little more than a skull with a wisp of honied hair. The teeth in the skull's open mouth wear a kind of mouthguard, pasted over with the hex-pattern of the honeycomb.

Ick. Teeth-stuff.

There's no discernable reason for putting the heads in the boxes. No clear logic to it. No overtly religious methodology that I can see, with my layperson's eye. No indication whether the sound got into these yokels' heads and *made* them do these murders, or if the sound simply *let* them.

When I'm done at the boxes, I go into the house and make sure that no one else is home.

Perfectly normal house. No pagan symbols smeared in shit on the walls. No chandelier made of bones or mummified great uncle in the basement.

There's Weetabix in the cupboard, but little else to eat.

In the basement I find a gas can. I exit the house and top the can off by syphoning from the truck I find parked out front.

Then I pile the bodies up, head to head, their shoulders leaning against the stack of beehives.

I'm sorry for the bees, but I torch the bodies, boxes, and all.

It hides my part in tonight's events, but it doesn't burn out the sound.

The sound keeps going.

The sound lives directly under the boxes. It churns under there. Has for forever, I think.

Before I leave, stumbling out into the night, sore, scratched and stung, the sound tells me that there's plenty more places like this one.

I hate to hear it.

Dusk
Orlando
Blake Cr

Bower
Copen
Burnsville
Walke
Stop
Coger or
Knawl
Sadie
Gem P. O.
Lef
Delta or
Braxton P.O.
Napier
Bulltown
Jopp
Bonnie
Fallamill
Rollyson
Saltlick
Hermione
Heaters
Bridge
Fairbanks
Supply
Hettie
Lloydsville
Berry
Flatwoods
Corley
Gregory
McNutt
Hopkins
Milroy

T
O
N
Caress
Ka
Newvill
195
Morrisons
22

ton
Gillespie or
Palmer Sta.
Hoover
Hyer P. O.
Holly Jt.
Palmer
Tesla
Bakers
Levi
anfield
Centralia
Littlebirch
Custis or
Holstead
Prestonia
P. O.

Fox
8
ggy.

The Valley of the Yunwi Tsunsdi

Brian Keene

Centralia, WV

Location of Centralia, West Virginia (community in Braxton County)

Coordinates: 38°37′23″N 80°34′4″W

Country   United States
State   West Virginia
County   Braxton

Population:
- Total   14,523 (Braxton County)

First Epicenter Sighting
- January 1966

Percent Burn
- 58%

Don Bloom peered through the binoculars and resisted smacking the mosquito incessantly tickling the back of his neck. Although he was concealed amidst the forest's greenery, he couldn't risk moving and being discovered. Seven armed men lingered down in the valley below, and if Bloom gave his position away now, he'd never get what he came for. His legs and feet tingled with numbness, but he remained still. Barros was down there somewhere, inside one of the ramshackle buildings that made up this backwoods methamphetamine compound.

And if Barros was there, then so was Kandara.

"Tricky," Bloom whispered.

Bloom had tracked his quarry across the country, starting in El Paso, where he'd first learned that Barros—a mid-level stooge for a Mexican drug cartel—was no longer simply controlling Kandara, but had become a host for the entity instead. The trail had led him across the southern United States before veering north. Bloom had almost caught up with him in Chicago but arrived too late, finding only a massacre inside a crumbling tenement building where human beings lay strewn about, horrifically tortured and then butchered like livestock. Bloom had seen similar atrocities before, in places like Iraq, Cape Town, Mexico and elsewhere. He'd even been the cause of some of them.

He'd followed the trail of slaughter east, finally arriving in Braxton County, West Virginia. He'd followed Route 17, passing through something called the Elk River Wildlife Management Area, and along the shores of Sutton Lake. Along the way, he saw plenty of campgrounds, RV parks, public game lands, and other facilities for public recreation. What he didn't see was the rest of America. There were no McDonalds or Wal-Marts. No Pier 1 stores or trendy coffee shops. None of the endless, soulless doppelgangers that pockmarked every other place in the country. None of the things that made it all feel the same, as if each town in America was nothing more than a picture cut out of a magazine, with no history or personality of its own. He didn't see many places of employment, either. A few logging trucks rolled past, trundling down the road, but there were no factories or mills or mining facilities. He did pass a number of small farms, and a few auto repair garages, and a big red barn that had been turned into a flea market, but that was it. Bloom suspected that this part of the state relied on tourism from hunters, fishermen, boaters, campers and hikers for its economy.

At the far end of Sutton Lake, the road crossed Laurel Creek and led into the unincorporated little town of Centralia. A historic marker sign on the outskirts of the village indicated that it was the geographic center of West

Virginia, and thus its name.

In Bloom's mind, that marker was about the only notable thing in the town. Other than the small box houses typical of the rural countryside, the only landmarks were a set of A&O railroad tracks—which looked worn but still operational—and a local convenience store that was refreshingly not part of a regional or national chain. He'd followed in Barros and Kandara's wake past these, then turned left onto Barkers Run, at which point the trail led into the forest. He parked his truck alongside a small independent grocery store and restaurant, which sat next to a campground. A handmade sign in front of the store advertised convenience items, firewood, hunting and camping supplies, and live bait.

He'd hiked into the mountains, following a game trail, until he'd come across the meth-cook compound, nestled deep in a gloomy, narrow valley, and ringed on three sides by high boulder-strewn cliffs with trees growing at precarious angles from the rocky soil. A rutted dirt logging road led in and out of the location, and a security fence topped with razor wire and cameras capped that entrance. Completely contained inside the fence's perimeter, the compound itself was a collection of rundown trailers and prefabricated shacks, all in various states of disrepair. There was also an outhouse that probably wouldn't withstand another winter, a mud-splattered monster pickup truck with a large Confederate flag crudely painted on the hood, several four-wheel all-terrain vehicles, a half dozen motorcycles, and a bunch of heavily armed hillbillies milling around. Bloom had watched them carefully for several hours, noting their movements and routines, and trying to determine how many people were down there.

Now, as his muscles cramped from holding still and the insects began descending upon him in droves, he still couldn't be sure. He'd counted just under two dozen men, including the seven he was now watching. There were probably more, given the number of vehicles below. No women among them, at least not that he had seen. And no sign of Barros, either. Bloom knew he was there, nevertheless. Kandara's pall hung over the valley, an almost palpable form of dread that seemed to make the gloom and shadows stronger.

As far as security went, the hillbillies weren't sloppy. They walked the perimeter and seemed fairly alert—but neither were they professionals. If any among them were ex-military, they'd long since forgotten the finer points of their training. The surveillance cameras remained stationary. Bloom wondered if they were operational, or just for show. He bet on the former. Frowning, he debated his options.

"Tricky," he repeated.

A full-out assault wouldn't work. Bloom was outnumbered and outgunned. He could try to wait Barros out, but the possessed man might not make an appearance outside. Worse, if Kandara sensed Bloom's presence, he'd lose the element of surprise. So far, he'd remained hidden from the entity by means of a charm a woman in Indonesia had made for him—but the longer he lurked here, the riskier it became. He and Kandara had history together, after all. Sooner or later, the entity would sense him, like a bad case of unrequited love.

His thoughts immediately turned to Jill. He felt a gnawing sensation in his stomach, and his chest tightened. He took a deep breath, exhaled, and forced himself to focus.

Bloom decided to go back to his truck for more weaponry and ammunition. Then, he'd return here after dark, and methodically work his way through the compound. Hopefully stealth and training would triumph over numbers. If not...?

Then the world was doomed.

Although the older he got, the more Bloom was convinced that it was doomed regardless. But while he couldn't do anything about politicians or climate change or civil and social strife, he could do something about Kandara. He had no choice.

Kandara was all his fault.

He stood slowly, easing the kinks and cramps from his muscles. The mosquitoes buzzed at this disturbance, and Bloom gritted his teeth, still not swatting them. After circulation returned to his legs, he started back down the trail. When he was out of range of the compound, he smacked the annoying insects with relish.

***

The forest grew louder the further away he got from the compound. Insects and birds called out from the treetops and underbrush. A dove cooed in the trees overhead as he crept through the woods. It was a lonely sound, and it made Bloom's thoughts turn to Jill again.

Growing up on South Clinton Avenue in Trenton, New Jersey, Bloom had few options upon graduating high school. College wasn't going to happen. His parents couldn't afford it, his grades were merely average, and although he'd played baseball and football, he wasn't scholarship material. Instead, after a chance encounter with a recruiter at the mall, Bloom enlisted in the Army and two weeks after graduation, he was on his way to basic training. Before he left, he and Jill went to see Linkin Park at the Garden. When the concert was over, they made love in the back seat of his parent's car. She made him promise that he'd come home again. He swore to her that he would.

He hadn't seen her since.

When he closed his eyes, Bloom could no longer picture Jill's face, or remember how her long blonde hair had smelled or how she'd felt. Those memories belonged to another man. They belonged to PFC Don Bloom, riding from Kuwait City to Baghdad in an M-88 tank recovery unit with the rest of the 3rd Infantry's convoy back in March of 2003. Only a little over a decade ago and yet a lifetime away. Another life altogether. The war had been going well then, all things considered. Saddam's sons were dead, the military resistance had crumbled, and rumor had it that President Bush was about to declare mission accomplished. They'd be back home soon.

Instead, their convoy took an unexpected detour. A sandstorm had knocked them off-course in southern Iraq. Stranded in the desert and unable to communicate with the rest of the convoy, Bloom and his fellow soldiers had begun an arduous trek across the wastelands. Near the ancient village of Al-Qurna, which many believed was the site of the Garden of Eden, they were captured by the Fedayeen. The group's leader had revealed that he was the cause of the sandstorm, and they were all to serve as sacrifices to an entity known as Kandara. The Fedayeen believed that Kandara was a djinn, and that he would lay waste to the 3rd Infantry before they reached Baghdad. According to their leader, Kandara could only be summoned with pain, and fed with suffering and anguish. And so, he had proceeded to torture and kill each of them, until Bloom managed to break free and kill the Fedayeen's leader. He'd done so by torturing the old man in much the same manner as his friends had been tortured.

It was then that Bloom had discovered that—by completing the ritual and sacrificing the Fedayeen's leader, he had gained temporary control over Kandara. He'd used it to wipe out more Iraqi forces, until control of the entity had been usurped from him by a renegade group of occultists who had supposedly broken away from a shadowy organization known as Black Lodge.

Branded a deserter and a criminal, Bloom had crisscrossed the globe, swearing allegiance to no nation, no flag, and no government, believing in nothing except his own abilities, and doing nothing except learning more about Kandara and tracking the monster and its handlers down, so that he could make amends for what he'd done in the desert. In that time, he'd discovered that the old man had been wrong about a number of things. Kandara was no mere demon or djinn, but instead a supernatural entity that had existed before the universe itself, one of several such beings, known collectively as the Thirteen.

After Iraq, Kandara had shown up along the coast of Somalia, a lawless region shattered by years of rebellions, coups, genocide, and warring factions that was rife with thugs, criminals, terrorists, and mercenaries. But it was also a region undergoing an economic boom of sorts thanks to the efforts of modern-day pirates who sailed out to international waters where maritime laws didn't apply, captured ships, abducted their crews, and then held both the sailors and the vessels for ransom. When Bloom arrived, one group of pirates were instead sacrificing their captives to Kandara. The land's suffering and strife, combined with the regular sacrifices, made the creature that much stronger. Bloom had managed to shut down the pirate ring, but Kandara— and his masters—had escaped. He'd followed them to Nigeria, Syria, and elsewhere. Ultimately, that trail had led to Mexico, where Kandara had grown fat and sated on all the suffering and murder committed by various warring drug cartels. Control of the entity had changed as well. Kandara apparently no longer required handlers. This new development had been a surprise to Bloom. He hadn't known that the entity could hide inside of people. Nor was he sure why it would choose to do so. Currently, Barros was the host— but Barros wasn't in charge. Kandara was using him as a vehicle. A car made of flesh and blood. A meat suit to hide inside, perhaps until it grew strong enough to manifest without being challenged.

What Bloom didn't understand was why the entity was waiting? Conventional weapons couldn't beat it. Black Lodge was compromised. Other than himself, was there anyone on Earth who could still challenge Kandara?

***

Levi Stoltzfus sat at a table in the corner of Centralia's lone restaurant and perused a menu. He was bemused to see both scrapple and hog maw listed as available. He glanced up at the waitress, whose nametag identified her as Lisa, and smiled.

"How is your scrapple?"

She snapped her chewing gum. "We make the cornmeal ourselves. You'll feel like you're back home."

"How do you know I'm not from around here?"

"Your accent. I'm guessing Pennsylvania or Ohio, right?"

"Correct. Marietta, Pennsylvania."

"Is that near Philly?"

"Sort of. It's in Lancaster County."

Her pencil hovered over her notepad. "Well, you'll love our scrapple. The other Amish hereabouts swear by it."

"Oh, I'm not Amish. At least, not anymore."

Lisa blinked, clearly studying his outfit—black pants and shoes, a white, button down shirt, suspenders, and a wide-brimmed straw hat, which he'd sat on the empty seat next to him.

"I'm sorry," she said. "I saw your beard and how you were dressed, and I just assumed…"

"No, I just prefer the simple way of dress. I guess old habits die hard."

"Is that why you rode up in that buggy?"

Levi shrugged. "Cheaper than an SUV."

"I know that's right!" Lisa laughed. "Well, I'm sorry for assuming. My momma always said, 'if you assume something you make an ass out of you and me.' She was full of wisdom like that."

"My father had a similar saying," Levi replied. "And you've convinced me. I'll take the scrapple."

"And to drink?"

"Water please."

"You want a slice of lemon with that?"

He nodded. "Please. Thank you."

"Coming right up."

Lisa bustled off with his order, and Levi glanced around the establishment. Half of it was a general store. The other half was a restaurant. He sat in front of a large window, giving him a view of both the door and the outside. His horse, Dee, and his buggy were both parked along the curb. Dee was tethered to a telephone pole. He'd been here ten minutes and had yet to see a car pass by. Given the scarcity of traffic, he was fairly certain she'd be okay out there.

He wondered if the same could be said for the rest of the town.

Levi was on his way north after a long trip. In the last month he'd been to the small West Virginian town of Brinkley Springs, where he'd fought a host of demonic revenants. After helping the townspeople, he had continued on to the Edgar Cayce Association for Research and Enlightenment headquarters in Virginia Beach. While their library was renowned as one of the largest collections of metaphysical studies and occult reference works in the world, there was a second collection—one not available to the general public— that held an eighteenth century German copy of King Solomon's *Clavicula Salomonis*, which Levi had made a copy of.

Heading home, Levi had stuck to the back roads since there was no way to take Dee and the wagon on the highways. He'd intended to pass by Centralia, but he'd felt a strange psychic pull as they approached the town. Parking along the side of the road, Levi had hopped down from the buggy and investigated, going off into the underbrush and nearby forest. As he walked, he held both hands out at his sides, palms down. Then he closed his eyes, took a deep breath, and held it, listening to the pulse of the land…

…and found that heartbeat to be erratic and weak.

"This is bad ground," Levi muttered. "The ley line is infected."

He'd patted the pocket over his left breast and felt the reassuring bulge of his dog-eared and battered copy of *The Long Lost Friend*. An heirloom, the book had been passed down from his grandfather to his father, and then to Levi. The front page was inscribed: *Whoever carries this book with him is safe from all his enemies, visible or invisible; and whoever has this book with him cannot die without the holy corpse of Jesus Christ, nor be drowned in any water, nor burn up in any fire, nor can any unjust sentence be passed upon him.* It was an unabridged edition; unlike the public domain versions one could find online. Those were watered down. This was the real thing. It had kept him safe many times. He prayed it would do so again now.

Sighing, he'd climbed back into the buggy and ridden into town, studying the houses and surroundings, looking for anything out of the ordinary, any sign of evil influence, any symptom that would allow him to diagnose whatever spiritual disease was sickening this place. Instead, he'd seen only human ills—despondence and poverty and plastic bottles and cigarette butts tossed along the roadside. Levi often mused that if the human race ever became extinct, far-off alien archeologists would one day arrive on the planet and the only artifacts they'd find were plastic bottles.

Arriving at the restaurant, Levi had decided to pause for a bit, break his fast, and try to get a feel for things there.

His mind wandered as he waited for his meal to arrive. He wondered if any of the local Amish that Lisa had mentioned were originally from Pennsylvania. Then his thoughts turned to his family. He'd left them in disgrace, years ago. Levi worked powwow—a form of both folk medicine and folk magic— just as his father had done, and his grandfather before him. Growing up, he'd watched as people came to his father seeking medical assistance. The patients varied from the elderly who remembered the old ways, the poor who didn't have health insurance or couldn't afford to see a doctor, and people who'd forsaken the mainstream medical establishment in search of a more holistic approach. He dealt with everything from the common cold to arthritis. Occasionally, he was called upon for more serious matters; stopping bleeding or mending a broken bone. When Levi was old enough, he'd begun to practice as well. But powwow was a magical discipline, just like any other, and once in a while, its practitioners were charged with doing more than helping the sick or curing livestock: supernatural threats rather than biological. In his eagerness to fight those threats, Levi had incorporated other forms of occultism and magical schools into his efforts. Doing so had led to tragedy—a horrific night that he didn't like to think about.

He hadn't seen his family since.

Levi always walked his road alone, a stranger to everyone except his God and himself.

Darkness settled upon him, matching the deepening gloom outside. Levi knew that sinking into depression would not serve him, but sometimes it was so hard to fight. He glanced around the restaurant, desperate for a distraction. He focused on the plastic placemat on the table in front of him. It was filled with advertisements for local businesses. He read each one twice. One—an ad for a place called Little People Daycare—sparked a memory. Something he'd read about in his library back home.

Folkloric belief in little people had spanned human cultures throughout the world's history, particularly in places like Ireland, the Philippines, Diego Garcia, Greece, and the Hawaiian Islands. But it occurred to Levi that the Native Americans had told of a race of little people who had inhabited the very Appalachian mountain range that Centralia was a part of. Such Native American folklore wasn't limited to this region, of course. The Crow Nation had legends of the Nirumbee—ferocious, demonic dwarves who lived beneath Montana's Pryor Mountains, and were depicted on local petroglyphs. The Umatilla tribe of Oregon told of little people they called Itste-ya-ha. The Sioux had numerous tales of a tribe of little people who lived on a mountain in South Dakota, near the junction of the Vermillion and Missouri rivers. In 1804, explorers Lewis and Clark had even reported an encounter with these same mysterious inhabitants, describing them as "devils with very large heads, about eighteen inches high, and very alert to any intrusions into their territory."

That description seemed to be common across North America, including right here in Appalachia, where the Cherokee said the Yunwi Tsunsdi lived. Like the little people mentioned by other Native American tribes, the Yunwi Tsunsdi were said to stand no more than twenty inches tall, had horns on their heads, and were frighteningly territorial. But it was also said that they could judge a person's sincerity and intent and would often grant spiritual insight or offer help and assistance, if needed.

Levi did not doubt the tales. In his experience, folklore and legends most often had a basis in truth. And there was physical evidence as well, including burial mounds in Tennessee, West Virginia, Kentucky and Pennsylvania, all of which had contained the skeletons of what were first thought to be children, but were later proven to be adults.

His reverie was interrupted as Lisa brought his water. He thanked her and then glanced up as a bell over the door rang. Another patron walked in and glanced around furtively. He was a young man, maybe late-twenties or early-thirties. Levi surmised he was most likely ex-military. He still carried himself with the telltale gait and stance of someone who served, but his hair, while still cropped close, and his beard were both just a little too long to pass an inspection. The newcomer was dressed in camouflage. His knees had soil stains, as if he'd recently been kneeling in dirt, and there were dead leaves stuck to the bottom of his boots.

The most interesting thing about the newcomer was his aura. It indicated despair and desperation and fear—but it also marked him as a fellow practitioner. Levi wondered which master the young man served, and which path he walked.

Lisa returned with Levi's scrapple as the fellow occultist approached the counter. As Levi picked up his fork, he overheard the young man order a hamburger and a bottle of water to go. Then he stood back from the counter and glanced around the restaurant again. Levi met his eye, smiled, and nodded at the seat across from him.

The young man frowned.

"There are plenty of empty seats, of course," Levi said, "but if you're interested in passing the time until your order is ready...?"

The frown deepened, but slowly, the newcomer approached. He eyed Levi, sizing him up, and then slid into the booth.

"Thanks, Mr...?"

"You may call me Levi. Levi Stoltzfus."

"Don Bloom." He stuck out his hand.

Levi put his fork down, wiped his hands with his napkin, and then shook.

"Is that your real name, Don?"

Suspicion flashed in the young man's eyes. "Why wouldn't it be?"

"Because names have power. That seems like something you should know already."

"Listen, pal. No offense, but I don't know what you're talking about."

Levi ate a forkful of scrapple and sighed in contentment. It really was exemplary, and the taste made him a little homesick. He swallowed, then looked at Bloom again.

"I think you do know what I'm talking about."

Bloom slid across the seat and started to rise. Levi motioned with his fork.

"Please. Hear me out. Give me until your burger is ready. If you don't like what I have to say, you can leave. Fair?"

Bloom remained sitting. "What do you have to say? What's this about?"

"I'm an observer. And because of that, I can tell you that there's something wrong with this town. Something most people wouldn't believe. But I suspect you will. And I can offer something up front that might make you listen to what I have to say."

Bloom hesitated. "Go on."

"Did you serve with a Donny Osborne?"

"How the hell do you know that? Who are you, really?"

"Just a short time ago, I was in Brinkley Springs, Virginia. I met Mr. Osborne and assisted him with a problem there. He mentioned his time in the military, and told me about the men he'd served with, including a Donald Bloom."

"Bullshit."

"He told me he missed his friends. Particularly you. He said you were captured by the renegade remnants of Saddam Hussein's Fedayeen, tortured, and then, after being rescued, you went AWOL somewhere inside the country. Nobody was sure why, or what happened to you after that. He'd heard different rumors—that you had crossed the border into Jordan and became a smuggler, or that you were working for a private security contractor, or dozens of other mindless speculations. He was pretty sure that none of them were true."

Grunting, Bloom crossed his arms.

"Let me tell you a little about myself," Levi continued, "and why I'm here. Perhaps it matches up with why you are here. If I'm right, then two are better than one."

"I work alone."

Levi nodded. "As do I. But I believe in providence."

"I don't."

"Humor me. It was providence that I met your friend. Maybe our paths have crossed for a reason."

Bloom shrugged. "You've got until my order is ready. Say what you've got to say."

Levi did.

And when he was done, Bloom shared as well.

***

"I'm still not sure about this," Bloom said as he collected his gear from the truck.

"After everything I revealed?" Levi gestured in exasperation. "I was able to tell you things about Kandara and the Thirteen that you didn't yet know."

"No, not that." Bloom shook his head. "I'll admit, you know your shit, Mr. Stoltzfus. More than anyone else I've met. And it's nice...having somebody to talk to about this kind of stuff. This life is lonely."

"It is. Which is why it will be nice to work with someone again."

"That's my point." Bloom holstered a handgun to his right hip, a combat knife on his right leg, and hoisted an AR-15. "Listen, you can obviously handle yourself when it comes to all this supernatural stuff, but Barros was bad news even before Kandara possessed him. These drug cartel guys don't fuck around. They're soldiers. And you're not."

"Ah, but that's where you are wrong. I am God's soldier."

Bloom snorted. "You ever have somebody bleed out in your arms on the battlefield?"

"Yes. Many times."

Bloom smirked. "Oh, yeah? Who?"

"The first was a girl named Becky."

Bloom paused, taken aback. "The first?"

Levi nodded. "I'll speak no more about her. The last was a partner named Dez. There was no blood left in him when he was done. None. So, to answer your question, Mr. Bloom, I have never served my country. I have never been conscripted by our government. But I am enlisted in an army nevertheless, and I serve and protect much more than a single nation or political philosophy."

Bloom studied him carefully. Levi wasn't physically imposing, but his eyes—they hinted at pain and horrors seen but never spoken. Bloom had seen eyes like that before. He saw them every time he looked in the mirror. Sighing, he unholstered his sidearm and offered it to Levi.

"You'll need this."

Smiling, Levi shook his head. "No thank you. I don't like guns."

"Maybe I didn't make myself clear. These guys are armed to the teeth."

"So am I."

"What…do you know some Amish karate or something?"

Levi winked. "Something like that. It's called powwow."

He turned and approached his horse and buggy. Bemused, Bloom followed him. Levi clambered up into the back of the buggy and pulled a dirty canvas tarp off a long wooden box.

"Can I come up?" Bloom asked.

Levi nodded. As Bloom climbed onboard, Levi lay the tarp aside. A bundle of what looked like dried weeds and twigs wrapped in duct tape sat atop the padlocked box.

"What's that?" Bloom pointed.

"A charm against livestock theft. It keeps Dee safe when I'm gone."

"That's your horse's name?"

"Indeed. I named her after John Dee. An old friend of the family."

"Wait...Doctor John Dee? The occultist?"

"The same. My line goes back a long way, Donald. So does Dee's. I've had her since she was a foal. Her family have aided my family for centuries. I'll tie this bundle around her bridle, and no harm will befall her while we are gone. But first..."

He knelt and unfastened the padlock. Bloom noticed a number of charms and sigils carved into the box, including a prominent one on the lid.

I.

N. I. R.

I.

SANCTUS SPIRITUS

I.

N. I. R.

I.

SATOR

AREPO

TENET

OPERA

ROTAS

"I recognize the top one," Bloom said, "but what's that below it? Satyr?"

"Sator," Levi corrected him. "It's a powwow benediction against evil."

He opened the box and rummaged through it. Bloom saw an assortment of books, an electronic tablet, vials of oils, candles, a knife, wooden matches, a cigarette lighter with a cross emblazoned on its side, a copper bowl, plastic freezer bags filled with various dried plants and roots, a peanut butter jar filled with what looked like locust shells, a small black leather bag, a compass, and more. Levi pulled out a black cloth vest and put it on. He selected a few other items from the chest and put them in the vest's pockets. Then he shut and locked the box again.

"You ready?" Bloom asked.

"Almost." Levi bowed his head and murmured a prayer. "The cross of Christ be with us. The cross of Christ overcomes all water and every fire. The cross of Christ overcomes all weapons. The cross of Christ is a perfect sign and blessing to our souls. Now I pray that the holy corpse of Christ bless us against all evil things, words, and works."

He looked up at Bloom again. "Now I am ready."

"I still think you ought to take one of my guns. And speaking of which, we should get off the street before somebody sees me carrying this rifle and gets the wrong idea."

Levi gestured at the forest. "Lead on."

***

"There's a few things I still don't understand," Bloom said quietly as they made their way through the darkness, following the narrow, winding game trail.

"Such as?"

"Well, these ley lines, first of all. What are they?"

"You know the latitudinal and longitudinal lines on a map?"

Bloom nodded.

"Well, ley lines are the supernatural version of those. They crisscross the Earth in a grid pattern, carrying psychic energy. In old times, civilizations built their megaliths and holy sites on them. Stonehenge, for example, and the Great Serpent Mound here in America, were both constructed atop ley lines."

"Why?"

"Think of it like recharging a battery."

"And one of these lines runs through this area?"

"Correct," Levi replied. "It's fascinating, really. It connects with other towns also named Centralia. One near my home, as a matter of fact. But Kandara's cult have done something. They've somehow poisoned the ley line. I don't know if it was intentional or just a byproduct of their presence in this place, but I need to fix that. Otherwise, bad things will happen."

"How so?"

Levi frowned. "Imagine the ley line as a blood vessel, flowing through a body. Infection sets in. If untreated, it begins to spread throughout the body.

Then what happens?"

"You die a horrible and painful death."

"That's exactly it. The regions that the ley line flows through would begin to see an increase in supernatural activity, as well as violence and the worst parts of human nature. Ultimately, the infection would kill everyone along the ley line. And if it spreads to other ley lines…"

"I get it," Bloom said. "I still don't understand the part Barros plays in all this, either. The old man who captured us in Iraq…he summoned Kandara."

"More likely he simply freed the entity from its imprisonment and brought it to our level."

"Whatever. He was Kandara's handler. Then I was for a while. Then, when it got loose, it went through various other controllers. But I never saw it possess one of them before."

Insects sang out around them. Far off in the distance, a coal train rumbled.

"Perhaps Kandara is afraid of you," Levi suggested. "From what you've told me, you've been a tenacious opponent, hounding its trail."

"I'd like to think so, but I'm just one man, Levi."

"Ah, but a determined man. And now we are two, rather than one."

Bloom shifted his rifle from hand to hand, flexing his joints. "Yeah, but that still doesn't explain Barros."

"Do you speak Portuguese or Spanish?"

"I know enough Spanish to get drunk or get laid or start a fight, but that's about it."

"The surname Barros comes from the Spanish and Portuguese word barro, which means clay or mud."

"And…?"

"I suspect the Barros you knew no longer exists. He is a construct, nothing more. A homunculus made of flesh rather than clay or mud. A vehicle for Kandara to move about more easily in, without attracting attention."

"Yeah, I figured the same thing. But why? Why does Kandara feel the need to hide?"

Levi paused before answering. "If I had to make an educated guess, I'd say the entity is close to achieving full strength. Its time is close. And Kandara knows you are still searching, so it's hiding until it can reach full power. How big was it the last time you saw the creature?"

"I don't know. About the size of a cow, I guess?"

"From everything I've read, Kandara was always depicted as a large cloud, blotting out the sky. I would guess that is its final form."

"How does something the size of a cloud…or the size of a horse for that matter…fit inside a man?"

"Barros is no longer a man. Remember that when we face him."

"Yeah, but that doesn't explain how Kandara would fit inside what's left of Barros."

Levi shrugged. "He's bigger on the inside than he is on the outside. Like a Tardis."

Bloom blinked. "You know Doctor Who?"

"Of course!" Levi smiled. "Tennant is still my favorite Doctor."

The coal train faded. The insects grew silent.

"Ut nemo in sense tentat," Levi whispered, "descendere nemo. At precedent spectaur mantica tergo. Hecate. Hecate. Hecate."

"What's that?"

"A powwow benediction against evil. Let us hope it will be enough to protect us and the people of this region."

Bloom frowned. "What people? That town was practically deserted. I think the only time the population swells is during tourist season. Unless you're counting deer, squirrels and turkey."

"There are other residents of this area besides the people and wildlife of Centralia," Levi said. "I have felt their eyes on us for the last two miles or so."

"Who?"

"The denizens of the forest. There are all sorts of tales about little people throughout the Appalachians."

"Little people? You mean like dwarves or leprechauns or some shit?"

"Not leprechauns per se, but certainly the source of the legends about them."

Bloom smirked. "Tell them we're not after their Lucky Charms."

"You don't believe?"

"I've seen a lot of stuff since the war, Levi…stuff that I know you'd understand. But I draw the line at leprechauns. I might change my mind if one jumped out and bit me, but otherwise…?"

Levi smiled placidly. "Well, let's hope it doesn't come to that."

***

They crouched in the undergrowth, staring down at the compound.

"Two sentries there at the gate," Bloom whispered. "My guess is they're standing watch in shifts."

"That's not so bad," Levi replied. "The others are probably sleeping or otherwise indisposed. We can handle two guards."

"It's not the guards I'm worried about." Bloom pointed at the security cameras. "We've still got to get around those without being seen or setting off an alarm."

"Leave that to me." Levi closed his eyes and bowed his head, as if in prayer. He murmured something under his breath, in a language Bloom didn't understand. Despite the cool of the night air, beads of sweat broke out on Levi's forehead. He began to tremor slightly. Then, after another moment, he sighed, opened his eyes, and nodded at Bloom. "Taken care of."

"What did you do?"

"A simple illusion, really. The cameras won't see either of us. We could stand in front of them and wave, but they won't register our presence."

Bloom studied his bearded companion. Levi's expression and tone were sincere.

"Can you do the same trick with the guards?"

Levi shook his head. "I could, but that is a bit more involved, and I'm afraid I don't have everything I need to make it effective."

Bloom patted his knife. "I do. But before I go down there, you swear those cameras are out?"

"No. As I explained, they are still functioning properly. They simply won't show us to whoever is watching the footage."

Bloom stared at him for another moment. Levi returned the gesture. Neither man blinked. Finally, Bloom sighed and set aside his AR-15.

"Bring this along with you, when I signal. Okay?"

Levi nodded. "What will your signal be?"

"I'll wave at you from the gate."

"Understood."

Rising from his crouch, Bloom crept forward, inching quickly down the sloped hill. Vines and brambles tugged at his combat boots and low-hanging branches brushed against his skin. A tangle of raspberries caught the holster of his handgun, and he absentmindedly picked a few and popped them into his mouth. He felt a burst of energy. Probably psychological, but he'd take whatever he could get. He picked and ate a few more as he moved. Red juice stained his lip.

Once again, Bloom was struck by how still the forest was near the compound. After dark, the woods should have been a cacophony of insects, frogs and other creatures singing out in their nocturnal choir, but instead, it was as if a blanket of silence had been thrown over the area. Although he walked swiftly and stealthily, it seemed to him that his footfalls sounded as loud as gunshots. If so, however, the sentries didn't seem to notice.

As he approached the valley floor, Bloom caught a glimpse of movement in the greenery to his right. When he turned his head, there was nothing there other than a bush of some kind. Frowning, he listened, but heard no telltale rustling that would indicate an animal, nor did he see any eyes reflecting back at him in the dark.

One of the guards coughed, and then lit a cigarette. Insects flitted around the tiny orange glow. The sentry waved them away with his hand, then coughed again. He muttered something, but Bloom couldn't make it out.

Bloom was about to creep forward again when the bush parted and a small, humanlike figure emerged in front of him. It stood about twelve inches, and stared up at him with an expectant expression. It was completely naked, but had no visible genitalia. Its skin seemed to blend with the surroundings like that of a chameleon. It tilted its head, eyes glinting in the dark. He gaped in astonishment, and was about to speak, when the creature held one tiny finger to its lips, indicating silence. Bloom slowly nodded in understanding.

The tiny person disappeared back into the bushes. They swayed and rustled as the creature closed the distance between him and the guards. Then, it popped out of the greenery and stood before them, chittering loudly.

The sentries pointed their weapons, but didn't fire. They glanced at each other in confusion and disbelief.

"Que demonios…"

Watching from the shadows, Bloom fought the urge to laugh as the tiny figure strutted back and forth, hands on its hips. The men continued to stare, clearly stunned. Then, the thing spat at them and ran back toward Bloom.

Tensing, Bloom pulled his knife from the sheath.

The men pursued the creature, crashing and blundering through the underbrush. It dashed past Bloom and plunged into the forest. Bloom let the first guard go by, then silently slipped behind the second guard. He wrapped his leg around the man's leg, pulled his forehead back with his free hand, and quickly cut his throat from left to right. There was a momentary delay, then Bloom's hand and wrist turned warm and wet as the cartel goon's blood bubbled and then jetted from the wound. The man dropped his weapon and clawed feebly at his spurting neck. Bloom slid him gently to the ground, kicked his gun away, and crept after the other.

He caught the second sentry at the edge of the forest. The man had tossed his cigarette butt aside and was scanning the tree line, sweeping his weapon slowly back and forth, looking for a target. There was no sign of the creature. Bloom slipped behind him, knife at the ready, when his foot came down on a fallen branch. The snap sounded like a gunshot in the silence.

Startled, the guard turned. His eyes went wide when he saw Bloom. Snarling, he raised his weapon. Bloom dropped his knife and charged, grabbing the rifle barrel and thrusting it up and away from him. Then he stamped down on the man's foot before he could fire a shot. The attack had no effect, given the heavy boots that the guard wore. His opponent swung the rifle, trying to hit Bloom with the stock, but Bloom stepped backward, pulling the man with him. Both toppled over, Bloom on the bottom. They glared at each other. The sentry's breath smelled of cigarette smoke and something else—something sour and rotten.

"Puta," he spat.

Grimacing, Bloom leaned his head forward and bit down on the man's nose, working his jaws, trying to get as much purchase as he could. His opponent squealed, but the sound was muffled given their proximity. Blood welled up in his mouth. Bloom grew nauseous at the taste but kept hold, pressing his teeth together. Then, he wrenched his head aside with a savage twist, and spat out the severed nose.

The man reeled backward on his haunches, and tensed up. The veins in his neck stood out like steel cables. He drew breath to shriek, but before he could, Bloom sprang up, wrapped his hands around the sentry's throat, and squeezed. The man's eyes bulged. Grunting, Bloom leaned forward and pinned his opponent beneath him, driving his knee into the man's abdomen. He squeezed tighter, shaking at the effort, and didn't let up until the guard went limp.

He stared down at those eyes, and watched the sentry die.

Then he listened.

There was no noise from the compound. No cries of alarm or the sound of running feet. But there was a noise from the forest. He glanced up, alert, as the little creature returned, leading Levi by the hand. The former Amish man studied the scene, expressionless.

"Are you injured?"

Breathing hard, Bloom spat blood and shook his head. "I see our friend found you, too?"

Levi nodded. "Do you still draw the line at believing in leprechauns?"

"That's no leprechaun. I'm guessing it's one of the…what did you call them?"

"Yunwi Tsunsdi."

The small figure reacted to the name, chittering softly and nodding.

"It recognizes the term," Levi observed, "although I suspect it has been a long time since it has heard those words spoken."

"What's it saying?" Bloom asked.

"I don't know. But I sense an urgency about it. This little one is troubled. His aura is…"

The creature let go of Levi's hand and hurried toward the compound. About halfway to the security fence, it turned and motioned at the two men to follow. They glanced at each other.

"It's helped us so far," Bloom said. "I guess it wants to show us something."

He bent and retrieved his knife, and used his shirt sleeve to wipe the blood and raspberry juice from his chin. Then he hurried after Levi, who was following their new friend.

The Yunwi Tsunsdi stopped when it reached the fence, and pointed at a prefabricated shack near the center of the darkened compound. The structure was larger than the other buildings around it. A domed dusk to dawn light glowed softly above it, suspended from a pole. Two more sentries guarded the closed door.

"Must be something inside there he wants us to find," Bloom guessed.

"Kandara," Levi whispered.

"Probably. He's close. I can feel him, hovering. Like when you know you're sick, and you can feel it inside of you? That's what it's like."

Levi nodded. "I can feel his presence, too. It hangs over this entire valley. The infection in the ley line is beginning to spread."

"How do we fix it?"

"I'm not sure. I would have to read up on the subject. There are a number of books on my Kindle, and in my library back home, but obviously I don't have access to those right now. I suppose we start by seeing what's inside that building."

Bloom gazed up at the razor wire strung across the top of the fence. "No way we're climbing over that. And I don't have any wire cutters. We'll have to circle back to the gate. Hopefully, they haven't noticed the guards are missing."

"If they had, we'd have heard it by now." Levi closed his eyes and gripped the chain links with his fingers. "And we don't need a wire cutter."

The magus murmured something in a language Bloom didn't recognize. He remained crouched by the fence for a full minute. Then, he took his hands away and opened his eyes. The links glowed orange.

"Can I borrow your knife?" Levi asked.

Bloom handed it to him. Levi used the blade to push the glowing part of the fence, which parted and fell away like warm taffy. Then he stood up, moved away from the smoking links, and handed the knife back to Bloom.

"Careful," he warned. "It's hot."

"That's a neat trick."

Levi shrugged.

Rifle at the ready, Bloom crept through the opening, careful not to let the melted metal touch him. Levi followed, along with their new companion. The little creature darted ahead, moving toward the shack. Bloom and Levi followed.

"I guess he's taking point," Bloom whispered.

The three crouched down behind a pallet stacked with oil drums and peered at the sentries guarding the shack. They stood still and watchful. Bloom got the Yunwi Tsunsdi's attention and motioned at the creature to stay put.

"See that corner of the shed, where that scraggly little bush is?"

Levi nodded.

"I'm going to sneak over there. When you see my signal, distract them.

Throw a rock or make a noise or something."

Levi nodded again. "I can provide a distraction."

Bloom crept out from behind their hiding place and approached the sentries from the side. He ducked around the corner of the shed and glanced back at the oil drums. Levi met his eye. Bloom nodded at him and readied himself. Levi raised his hands, gestured and contorted…

…and frogs fell out of the sky.

It wasn't a torrent or a downpour—only a dozen or so, localized directly over the guards. But the fall got their attention. The two men gaped in confusion, then glanced at each other. One of them pointed his gun at a frog as it hopped across his foot. Then he nudged it with the barrel.

The other guard drew a breath to speak, but before he could, Bloom slipped behind him and drove his knife into the base of the man's skull. Then, moving quickly, he let the corpse drop and lunged at the remaining sentry. His opponent raised his weapon. His finger slid toward the trigger. Bloom stabbed him in his throat. The man's eyes went wide, and he stumbled backward toward the door, taking the knife with him.

Bloom grabbed for him, but the dying guard was quicker. He squeezed the trigger, firing off a single round. The round kicked up dirt and rocks, but missed Bloom entirely. Then the man backed into the door and tumbled inside the shack.

"Shit!"

His cover blown, Bloom acted quickly, leaping over the fallen guards. He charged into the building, rifle extended, and fired at the first target who moved. The bullet punched through the man's chest, knocking him down. Bloom swung his weapon to the right and shot a second target. Then he hesitated, as he caught a glimpse of the scene.

It was like being in Iraq all over again.

The interior of the shed had been turned into a makeshift torture chamber. A steel workbench sat in the center of the room. Its surface was stained with blood. So were the vice attached to the tabletop and the tools that lay scattered across it—screwdrivers, saws, hammers, pliers and more. A small, red mass lay glistening in the center of the workbench, and it took Bloom a moment to realize the wet thing was the remains of a Yunwi Tsunsdi.

Two of the interior walls were lined with cages like a dog kennel. Many of them housed more of the little creatures. The Yunwi Tsunsdi looked starved and terrified.

There were three more opponents in the room. None of them had guns, for which he was glad, or this momentary hesitation would have gotten him killed. The first man held a bloody claw hammer, its tip covered with gore and matted hair. The second clutched a linoleum knife. The third was unarmed, concealed in shadow. Then the man stepped forward, grinning.

Bloom's eyes narrowed. "Barros."

"YOU KNOW BETTER THAN THAT," the thing inside Barros said. *"AFTER ALL, YOU WERE MY FORMER JAILER."*

"Kandara."

"IN THE FLESH. OR…AT LEAST THIS CURRENT FLESH."

The man holding the linoleum knife lunged, darting forward with an angry shout. Bloom shot him before he'd made it three steps. The attacker fell face first onto the dirty concrete floor. The knife skittered into a corner.

Before Kandara or his lone remaining minion could react, Levi and the Yunwi Tsunsdi rushed into the shack. The little forest person saw the state of its imprisoned kin and wailed. They, in turn, gripped the mesh of their cages and chittered.

"Are you okay?" Levi kept his eyes on Kandara as he spoke.

"I'm fine," Bloom replied. "The fat fuck over there is—"

"I know who it is. Kandara, smallest of the Thirteen."

"AND I KNOW YOU, AS WELL, LITTLE MAGUS! LEVI STOLTZFUS, SON OF…"

The entity trailed off.

"I guess you don't know me as well as you thought," Levi said.

"SUCH INSOLENCE! YOUR DEATH WILL BE SLOW. YOUR PAIN WILL BE A FEAST LIKE NO OTHER FOR ME. SMALLEST? THAT WOULD BE MEEBLE. I WILL SHOW YOU JUST HOW LARGE I CAN BE."

Barros's skin began to shift and swell, as if snakes were crawling around inside his veins. He threw back his head, arms stiff at his sides, and a black, inky cloud began to pour from his mouth and nose and ears, coalescing in the air above him.

Bloom raised his rifle and took aim, but the remaining cultist tossed the claw hammer. The missile flew through the air and struck him in the leg. Yelping, Bloom staggered backward. The man charged him, head low, fists balled. Bloom swung the rifle around, driving the stock into his attacker's shoulder. The guard reeled, and Bloom shot him in the knee. Then he put another in his head.

"The ley line," Levi said. "This is where they are…"

Kandara ran past them in Barros's body, fleeing.

Cursing, Bloom started to pursue him, but the Yunwi Tsunsdi grabbed at his pantleg and tugged. He glanced down at the creature. It stared up at him with a pleading, desperate expression. Then its mournful gaze turned to its captive kindred.

"Levi," he yelled, "can you help him free his people?"

When the occultist didn't answer, Bloom turned around. Levi knelt on the floor in the center of the room, peering down into a small, circular drain.

"What the hell are you doing?"

"This leads into the ley line. Whatever they were trying to achieve, they did it from here."

"Levi…" Bloom glanced out the door. Kandara had disappeared into the darkness. "He's getting away."

"He's already escaped. And without assistance, he'll be on the run for a while. He'll need to amass new followers. New victims. Our primary concern is here."

"Fuck that. I came here to stop Kandara!"

"And I was drawn here to take care of this. Go!"

Bloom hesitated for a moment. Then he turned to the door and ran outside. The compound was silent, and dark. He glanced around, looking for any sign of Kandara, but the entity had vanished. He jogged to the main gate, but it remained closed. Suspecting that perhaps his foe was still inside the compound, he waited, listening. Then he spotted something stuck to the razor wire atop the fence—a scrap of clothing and a bigger scrap of flesh. Kandara had scaled it, obviously, and escaped into the forest.

Sighing, he turned back to the shack, and hung his head.

When he reentered the building, Levi and the Yunwi Tsunsdi were opening the cages and helping the other tiny creatures down to the floor. The diminutive people cooed and embraced. A few wept. Bloom watched them and forget about Kandara for a moment.

"I thought you went after your prey," Levi asked, lifting another captive from its cage.

"He's gone. I'll have to wait until daylight to track him."

"Can you do that?"

Bloom nodded. "He injured Barros's body climbing the fence. There will be a trail of blood. Plus...I can sense him, once I get close."

"I would offer to go with you, but I'll have to tend to this."

"The ley line?"

Levi nodded.

"Think you can fix it?"

"No," the magus admitted, "but I suspect that the Yunwi Tsunsdi can. If they can show me how, then maybe I can repair the other locations."

"So, more traveling for you, too, then."

Levi smiled, but his expression was sad. "In this life we've chosen, Donald, it sometimes seems that traveling is all we do."

"Amen to that."

They stood quietly for a moment, watching as the Yunwi Tsunsdi were reunited. Then, Levi turned and walked outside. Bloom followed. The sky above the valley was turning from black to blue, and the stars were beginning to fade.

"The sun will be up soon," Bloom said. "Then I'll get after him."

"Sunrise has always been my favorite time of day. But it is seldom that I get to watch it, let alone watch it with someone else."

"I can hang out for a bit."

"That would be nice. I would like that."

"Yeah," Bloom admitted. "Me, too."

They walked outside the compound and climbed the valley slopes.

"Any idea where that poisoned ley line will lead you?" Bloom asked.

"Not really. But I have my suspicions. This isn't the only town named Centralia, and the others across the country seem to follow the line itself."

"That's a pretty weird coincidence."

"I don't believe in coincidence," Levi replied. "And you? Any thoughts as to where Kandara might flee to?"

Bloom shrugged. "Anywhere there's pain and suffering."

"The whole world then."

Bloom nodded.

"Well, who knows then?" Levi smiled. "Perhaps our paths will cross again, before our work is through."

They reached the top of a hill and sat together in silence, watching the sunrise, and enjoyed not being alone for a little while.

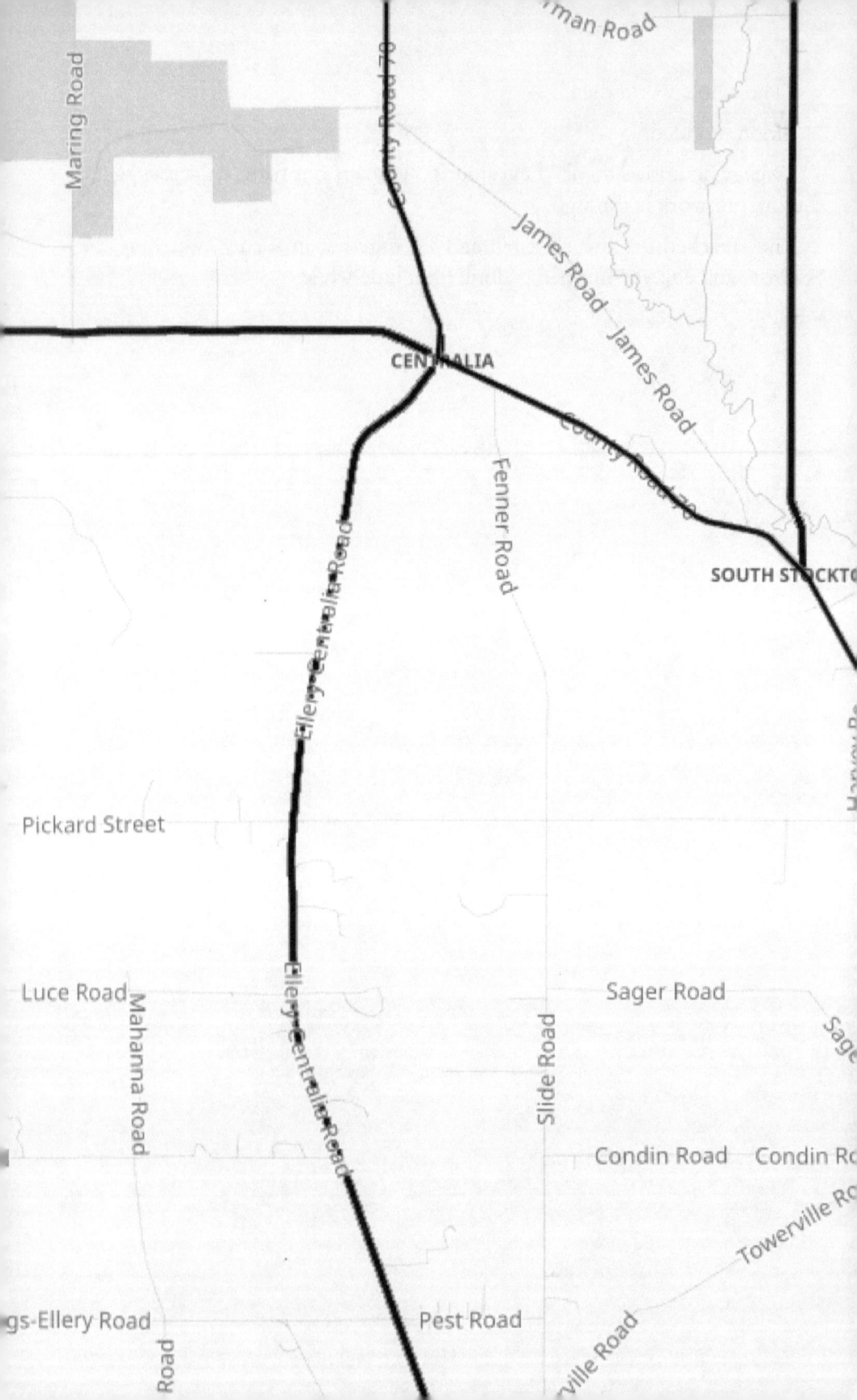

G.W. Bolt

and the Case of the Grabbed Ghost

Brian Quinn

Centralia, NY

Location of Centralia, New York (Hamlet of Stockton)

Coordinates: 42°18′9″N 79°21′5″W

Country   United States
State   New York
County   Chautauqua
Area
• Total   47.65 sq mi (123.41 km2)
Population
• Total   2,248
First Epicenter Sighting
• January 1970
Percent Burn
• 46%

There are many weird things in the world, and I am one of them. I'm actually a little beyond even the "average" borders of weirdness, because as far as I can tell, I'm the only thing like me in existence. I hope that's not true. I really do.

I write cases of mine down like this for a lot of reasons. First and foremost, I've been at this a long time and I don't know how long I'll be at it still, so I want all my facts and clues straight. My memory is good, but it isn't perfect. Something to do with not having a brain, maybe?

Second, if I ever am discovered by humanity I figure these books will be a good way to help me be understood and hopefully not be cut and broken apart in the name of science. Or worse, in the name of faith. Whoever got their hands on me first, actually. I'm sure they'd all line up to be the first to figure out what I am. I imagine there would be a lot of books written about me by people who don't know me, and I figure I should weigh in while I can. To be clear, I don't hold anything against these hypothetical people as I'm basically on the same mission as they would be - to figure out what's going on here with this guy. I just don't want to be torn apart or locked away in the process. After all I've seen in the 20th century, I really have a dim view of my chances if I am ever discovered. As shitty as my life can be sometimes - most times, really, - I do prefer being alive. And I am alive. I stress this so you understand – I am alive. I don't breathe, but I feel. I think, therefore I am.

Right? That's a rule that everybody knows. I think, therefore I am.

I think. Therefore. I am.

Apologies. I'm getting lost, freaking myself out. I'm not verbose at all, how could I be when I can't actually speak? Nor am I used to ordering my thoughts down like this. My earliest journals, especially as I taught myself to write, are pretty rough. I got better. I should burn some of those early journals, I guess. They are embarrassing. Better to put my best foot forward.

The case. The case. Let me write down the events before I forget anything-

I finished the last symbol that the spell required. What followed happened quick, and it worked. With a slight puff of air, the ghost I was hunting was solid, and he looked just as shocked as I was. It's rare this spell works for me and although I have theories about why that is, it's still surprising when they pop back into corporal existence. His pale, whitewashed eyes looked down at his body and he attempted to draw breath. I figure that was just left-over muscle memory from being alive, and I made a mental note to sketch the expression on his face later. You never know what will amount to something.

The ghost looked up at me as I approached.

"What are you?" he asked. Can you imagine that? This guy has been dead for who knows how long and I still freak *him* out. Must be the face. My face is just human enough to really screw with people.

What passes for adrenaline coursed through my body. I have no idea about that either. After all these years my best guess is that it's a psychic energy spike of some sort that resembles what I've read adrenaline feels like to you fleshy people. The idea of cutting myself open to see what it actually is appeals to me about as much as you cutting your head open to see what's causing a headache. Not happening, so I call it adrenaline.

Whatever it is, it makes me sloppy. A few notes of light music jingle out of my torso. Embarrassing, but this is what happens when you have a music box where your lungs should be. I reached out and grabbed the ghost with my right hand a little too hard, and I feel one of my finger joints ping with the stress. Normally this would send me into a panic, but, like a fool, I think I might have finally done something that would help explain my own existence. Over 80 years old and I still have my little delusions.

"Please. I don't understand what's happening. Where's Alba?" the ghost stuttered as I pulled him near. "I was sick....I think something bad has happened. Please!"

Even if I could answer him, which I can't, I wouldn't bother. Whoever this guy is he had a life, he was able to walk out amongst people on days other than Halloween without fear of getting ripped apart and studied. It seemed like he had love, with this Alba dame. Whether he lived a good or bad life it doesn't matter, that's all gone now and no amount of me feeling bad for him is going to help, so I don't. I'm the one with problems that matter and, like it or not, this leftover scrap of human can help me.

I pulled him close with my right hand and held up my little chalkboard with my left. The chalkboard is how I "speak" and it's a royal pain in the ass, but you try to get people to understand what you mean by hitting a few bars on a music box with only six notes. I pushed the chalkboard into his face and he looked from me to it and back again. He didn't answer and I didn't know how long this spell would last so I throttled him back and forth and hit his forehead with the chalkboard for emphasis.

He focused up and blinked at the chalkboard, but I could tell he didn't understand what was going on. Though I didn't feel bad then and still do not feel bad now, I could at least relate to the poor bastard. The ghost read what I'd written for a second time and then looked at me, his confusion deeper.

"I don't know what you're asking," he said. "I was right here a minute ago. Where is Alba?"

My metal eyelids fluttered in frustration. They do that sometimes, although I wish they would not. I released him and pulled a piece of chalk out of my trench-coat pocket. I didn't like letting go of him but I needed to get answers before he vanished and I need to write my questions down. My kingdom for a voice box.

I deal with these sort of frustrations all the time in my line of work. I hunt ghosts. I mean, I hunt a LOT of weird things that you would consider supernatural, but I focus mainly on ghosts and the various magical methods of communicating with them. There is the occasional sidetrack. I killed a mermaid off the coast of Staten Island, back in the 1980's. She was killing fishermen and pornographic movie producers. That's the sort of shit I run into from time to time. It can eat up a lot of time, running around dealing with things like vicious rogue mermaids, which is yet another reason I try to focus mainly on ghosts. Ghosts are tricky but you know what you're getting with a ghost. Communicating with them is the key, because I need answers that so far only the dead can help provide, but it is very hard. To get anything out of a ghost you have to stop just short of bringing them back to life, and you can only pull that trick off with maybe one in a hundred of them. It seems cruel, to be honest, but I have my own problems.

A ghost is only a memory, as far as I've found in my cases, and I've seen a lot of them. They aren't conscious beings. Grandma isn't standing next to you, whispering her oatmeal cookie recipe in your ear and telling you she loves you. Grandma is gone, bub. I've looked hard for Grandma and so far, no sign. But ghosts ARE real. People see them, although rarely enough that they get waved away in the light of reason. People who carry on about seeing ghosts are usually deemed kooks, but ghosts are real, and with the right mixture of gumption and magic, you can use that remnant of human soul to reach into the afterlife and rip the poor bastard right back to the land of the living for a question or two. About life. About death especially. Death, what it's like to be dead, and most importantly, how the fuck to stay away from death, preferably forever.

Yes, yes, yes. Ashes to ashes. Dust to dust. Everything that is born must die, for some cruel reason.

The thing is, I wasn't born. I was made. Not even from flesh and body parts, like a proper monster. I'm made out of steel, mostly. Some brass, some copper. My face is mostly brass, with those rather handsome copper inlays that suggest facial features. My eyeballs are copper, I think. I don't know how I can still use them to see through, because that's not how seeing works, but I see through them nonetheless. Which is just one more question about myself that I'm trying to get an answer to.

If you're reading this journal, something went really wrong for me. Or really right, but I don't have a lot of experience with that. Things going right isn't part of my day to day experience. What I get is fear. I live in fear. I am constantly terrified, though you couldn't tell by looking at me. I can't make expressions that convey fear. I spent some time trying to figure out how to waggle my copper eyebrows in an approximation of fear, but it just looks like I'm trying to be one of the Marx Brothers. I miss the Marx Brothers, by the way. They don't even play them on TV anymore. I have them on DVD, but it's not the same as stumbling across them on Channel 11 and getting sucked in.

I shouldn't be alive and I don't know how I came to be alive in the first place, so I'm always terrified. Look, when a regular person dies, it's understandable. As mind-blowing and repulsive as the concept of death is, most people know it's part of the deal. You're born and then you're placed on this conveyor belt that moves you through your years, mostly filled with predictable landmarks and visibly marked by your aging body. For you, most everything is ordered and on an established timeline. You know you're constantly headed toward your death, that at the end of that non-stop conveyor belt is total erasure from existence. All you know and all you love are going to fall into that black maw and be subjected to eternal oblivion. Gone, as if you never really existed at all. As if you were pointless from the get-go.

It's a shit deal, but you have time to get used to this idea and mostly you understand that you will die at an average time and usually because of a completely understandable cause. You silly scamps started coming up with religions just to try and take the sting away from the idea. Mostly, you've seemed to evolve to just not think about it most of the time. Me? I don't know *any* of the rules of my own existence. How am I alive? Do I have a soul? What keeps me alive? Am I my body? Am I more than that?

I don't fucking know. Rust sends me into a panic. If I spot a tiny rust flake on my body I can't help but think that if I scrape it away, I scrape away a bit of my soul.

I keep myself well oiled. Oil ain't cheap. Lotta cabbage. I steal it mostly, but sometimes I have to go online like everybody else. You should see my eBay rating, five stars across the board. I pay on time and leave good feedback.

Remember that, please, if you're looking to take me apart to see what makes me tick.

I'm rambling. I don't know how to express myself with words as well as I would like because I can't speak and I never interact with people. I have no practice.

Let me start at the beginning.

My name is George Washington Bolt, and I am a beer-drinking automaton. Let that shit sink in. Half of you are wondering what an automaton is. The other half is wondering how the blazes an automaton drinks beer. I'll clear both up for you.

An automaton is basically a robot before robots were a thing. Low rent robot. Something that moves in a few basic pre-determined motions, and usually made to look like a human being. A music box with a dancing ballerina is technically an automaton. You ever see that Tom Hanks movie, *Big*? Where a kid turns into an adult because he made a wish on a fortune teller machine? That fortune teller, Zoltar, is an automaton.

I've watched *Big* many times and I'm unsure how I feel about Automaton-American representation in that movie. I kid. Not about watching *Big* many times. I had a VHS copy back in the 1990's. I stole it, but only because renting movies is a problem for me. I could never waltz into a Blockbuster Video and check out the latest releases. Try signing up for a Blockbuster account when you have no ID, no credit card and no heartbeat. So, unless I was willing to break into a video store – super risky – I was always way behind on movies. Once streaming happened though! Whoa! I fucking love movies. All I had to do is figure out how to steal internet and now every night is Sundance at Casa De Bolt.

I am an automaton. I was created by a man named Charles Barris in 1933 in Centralia NY. I have pictures of him in my humble basement hideout. He's a handsome man with a swell head of hair, and sometimes I look at myself in the mirror and imagine that he based my face on his, but I don't know if that has any truth to it at all. I don't know much about my "father" as he died before I even realized that I was alive, but what I do know comes from the journals he left behind. It's where I got the idea for journals of my own, from my "dad." Barris was mainly a clock worker by trade, but he would occasionally dip into other projects. There was a jewelry shop on Main Street in Centralia that had a storefront sign that Charles Barris made for them in the 1920s. It's still there. It doesn't run anymore, but when it was new it had moving pieces shaped like diamonds that would dance across it hourly to music, as well as a metal woman who would open a box and pull out a pearl necklace. Her jaw would drop in excitement. Then the whole thing would reset for an hour. It was intricate and delicate and townspeople loved that sign, but that wasn't enough to keep it up and running once Barris died. Too expensive to find someone who had the proper skills to keep it going. Now it just sits there silently, above a Vape store of all things.

Sometimes, while everyone else is sleeping, I'll toss on my trench coat and hat and go look at that sign. It's actually the closest thing I have to family. Off the cob, right?

Corny, I mean. I have to remind myself to update my slang sometimes. I've been around the block a few times at this point.

G.W. Bolt, as I was referred to when I was referred to at all, was built at the request of a William Horrmann of New York City, who owned a beer company and wanted to have a "beer-drinking metal man" that he could use as a promotional tool to make his beer stand out at the end of Prohibition. The plan was to have men see if they could outdrink the mechanical man, a challenge that was very much tongue-in-cheek, but still quite effective. Mr. Horrmann rightfully assumed that all a certain type of man needed to pound beers was an excuse, and G.W. Bolt provided a fun excuse. G.W. Bolt would spend six years being transported around pubs and bars in the Northeast, successfully promoting Horrmann Beer and out-drinking all comers. I remember nothing of this time, which leads to me believe that I hadn't come alive yet. I regret this, because I would have liked to have the memories of my father and the experience of being in those bars. I don't hold any sort of grudge or bad feelings toward Barris, quite the opposite. If I am alive because of something he did, intentionally or not, then I am grateful to the man. The whole purpose of my being, the reason I do what I do, is because I quite like being alive and want to stay this way.

Charles Barris was constantly working on G.W. Bolt during the years it toured the drink halls. He maintained the automaton and repaired the frequent damage it suffered at the hands of rowdy drunks as well as upgrading the device with the experience he gained throughout the years. Originally, G.W. Bolt was seated and the only two parts of him that could move independently were its jaw and right arm which would lift a full glass of Horrmann Beer to his mouth and pour the alcohol down a copper tube into a hidden tank that would be emptied after the bar had closed. If I may say so myself, it's actually a pretty clever idea and I suppose I owe something to Horrmann for coming up with the notion.

Because of the endless attention and, dare I hope, *love* that Barris paid his creation, by the end of 1938, G.W. Bolt could stand on his own, walk with assistance, articulate both arms and neck, play the Horrmann Beer Jingle from an internal music box, and had a range of facial expressions. All powered through a meticulously designed and maintained mainspring, set into an internal, complex clockwork of Barris' own design. I have some of the drawings that Barris made in designing me. At first they creeped me out, like maybe the first time you had a doctor send a camera down your throat. All those wet, dark internal parts of your body that you'll never see with your own eyes. If you're lucky, I guess. I understand how intricate and delicate the work that Barris accomplished is, and I just dread the thought of a single internal spring popping loose. You can go see a doctor, at least. I worry that if I remove my chest plate to see what's happening inside me, the life will disappear from my body, and I'll tumble to the floor. Another pile of junk rotting away in the basement of a rotting house. Any time I've had to make even slight repairs on myself, it's been a hard-boiled proposition. It's a good thing I don't sweat.

Where does my "soul" live? What dare I alter on my body? There is no map. I'm off the edge of the map. Here there be monsters.

For G.W. Bolt, time was running out. Like all things that you humans love - friends, family, pets - the end was coming. By the beginning of 1938, G.W. Bolt had become too familiar of a figure and, despite its astounding construction, people lost interest in beating the metal man in beer drinking contests. Apparently, most drunks would just pretend to hump it to make their equally sloshed friends laugh. Mr. Horrmann was unwilling to pay the relatively high cost of keeping G.W. Bolt up and running if he was no longer a successful marketing gimmick, and the automaton eventually stopped working due to this neglect. Barris wasn't even allowed to work on it for free, according to his notes. Something, I was happy to read, that caused him some real distress. He cared about me. Why? I don't know. Maybe he knew what I was even back then. Maybe he knew I could live. Maybe he was an autistic man unable to let go of his creation. Yet another mystery to me, but he sometimes expressed affection for me in his journals, and he never had kids of his own.

I'm projecting. I learned that in a self-help book I stole when I was considering killing myself back in 1976. I do that from time to time, you see. I contemplate just ending it all. Why struggle and suffer throughout the decades if the only reward for my labors is death? But, and here is some irony for you, what if I *can't* die? What if I toss myself off a building, smash into a million itty bitty pieces and I still don't die? How horrible would that be?

In August of 1938, G.W. Bolt hosted his last drinking contest and found his new home collecting dust in the lobby of the Horrmann Beer Brewery on Staten Island. It was at this point that Charles Barris approached William Horrmann and made him an offer that was too good to pass up. Charles Barris would build an exact replica of G.W. Bolt, minus the internal clockwork, and give that to Mr. Horrmann so that he could continue to display his old mascot in his lobby, plus he would buy back the original G.W. Bolt at the same price Mr. Horrmann paid for him in 1933. Horrmann was only too happy to recoup his money, and G.W. Bolt went home with its creator to Centralia, NY.

I tried looking up that duplicate version of me, by the way. Nobody on the internet knows what happened to it. The brewery burned down in the 1960's, but it had been closed for years before the fire. I worry about that "brother" of mine. I fear he came alive too, but had no ability to move. Just sat there, frozen and terrified while the humans ignored him. I worry he was tossed into a scrap heap, unable to help himself out while the vermin nest in his innards. Or what if he was melted down and he felt every hot stinking moment of it? I still hope I can find him. It'll give me something to focus on besides myself.

Charles Barris continued working at home on G.W. Bolt to the point of obsession. Through the better part of a year, G.W. Bolt was restored and upgraded, although the extent of these upgrades is unknown even to me. Many of Barris' journals were lost to time and rot. I got what I could from them, but it's a spotty account. The plan was for this new G.W. Bolt to be unveiled at the 1939 World's Fair in Queens, NY. One newspaper account of the fair reports that Barris was very excited about showing the world what he had accomplished, going so far as to claim that the world "might not be ready" for what they would see. This is the part that gets me. Did he know? What did he do to me to bring me to life? Or was he just blowing smoke up his own ass to drum up interest? I have not been able to get a sense of the man through his rather sterile writings. He remains largely concealed from me. How well do you know your own father? Do you like what you know? I'll tell you this, you know he humped your mom and that's how you were made. You know that for sure.

G.W. Bolt would never appear at the World's Fair. In March of 1939, weeks before he was to unveil his creation to the public, Charles Barris died of a heart attack in his Centralia home. Childless, Barris' estate was distributed to various relatives, none who had an interest in the metal man. G.W. Bolt was crated up and stored in the basement of Barris' home, which was eventually foreclosed on by the bank and written off as a loss. G.W. Bolt was forgotten and left to rot in the basement of a rotting, forgotten home in the woods of Centralia.

This is where I come in. The real me. The alive me. I sat in that crate for years. Dark, cold and often wet. Then, something happened. Something so subtle that I can't even place my steel finger on when. I had a *thought*. I don't even remember what that thought was, but once I had it, I realized that I had actually been conscious for some time. I just didn't realize it. Wacky, right? You'll have to give me a pass on that one. I have no frame of reference. I was just….. waiting. Waiting for my creator to come and tell me what to do.

Thoughts led to movement and eventually I emerged from my moldy, soggy crate of a womb. I recall that I disturbed a particular comfortable family of rats. I crushed a baby rat with my metal foot, the squeal frightened me and gave me my first spoonful of what life had to offer. Confusion. Fear. It was 1955, my creator was dead and unable to give answers and I was all alone in an abandoned house with no idea of what to do next. No idea what I was.

I could, however, read, which is completely confusing to me. Why be born with the ability to read, you know? Equally confounding, I could understand the English language. I think in English as well. I don't understand any other languages, which I'm sure is a clue about my existence that makes no proper sense to me at all, even now. I'm not complaining. Being able to read saved me back then, as I hope being able to write will save my bacon in the future. Amongst the abandoned possessions that the Barris relatives couldn't be bothered to claim were journals and luckily some had even survived the years. Through these journals I found incomplete blueprints of myself and many scattered and often conflicting thoughts and notes. More questions than answers. Again, nothing I wouldn't get used to over the years.

It took a few years to get a grip. Imagine having to teach yourself the concepts of life and death, using only the stolen knowledge of a weird fleshy species that you're roughly based upon but not actually a part of. No lie, it sucks, brother. It's lonely. It didn't take long to figure out that revealing myself to humans was not a good idea. I tried early on. Like some cement-headed idiot I slowly worked up the courage to approach my first humans. Some drunk frat kids almost took me apart. I hid from them in an old abandoned refrigerator and pulled the door shut. I stayed in that fridge for a week, one of the benefits of not needing oxygen. By the time I snuck back home, I had a pretty good handle on how I would be received.

Side note - I recently saw the obituary for one of those college kids. He died at the age of 79. I don't feel any happiness at his death, just so you know. I don't want you to think I'm sitting here happy for humans to die. I want to stress that. I am not a vengeful thing. I'm alive, I'm just pointing out that he aged and died and I'm still here. As of yet, aging does not appear to be one of my problems.

So, unable to pass as human and scared to reveal myself, I stuck to the woods of Centralia, only going out at night to break into libraries and houses in search of any information that might help me solve the mystery. My early theories, of course, were not based on the supernatural. I didn't have a concept of the supernatural back then. At first I thought I was a human with various prosthetic arms and legs. And head. A prosthetic head. If I could laugh, I would.

Not knowing what makes me alive has made me something of a hypochondriac. I will take extreme measures to maintain my safety because I do not know what would happen if I replaced even a single bolt on myself. Where does my conscious live, and can I risk tinkering with my own mysterious innards to find out? Discovery was my original mission and I learned as I went. Things got easier. I got more confident. Mail order came into my life. I had to steal money, sure, but now I had access to books and with that came theories. I was clearly on the supernatural spectrum, that was undeniable. So it made sense to focus my efforts in that direction.

As the decades pass, I investigated more and more cases of unusual phenomena in an effort to learn about myself, eventually becoming something of an expert in the arcane and cryptic. Over the course of the past 60-odd years, I've faced all manner of supernatural and mystic threats, but very little that can shed light on my own existence. I take any crumb or hint as a victory to bolster my resolve and not just fold my cards. So, here I am, investigating every story or legend I can, occasionally fighting back against the darker forces of the universe, never stopping until the day comes that I knows what I am, and why. It sounds cooler than it is.

I feel things. A sense of touch, yes, but here I mean emotions. I feel them pretty much how I've come to understand that you do. I get lonely, but that's such a constant that it always hums in the background. I had a crush on a woman once, which was nice. I had broken into her house to steal a book on the occult her stupid husband bought at an auction. Turns out she was home when all my preparation stakeouts made me believe she wouldn't be. That'll happen. You humans are an unpredictable lot, but it's something you learn to work with if you don't want to lose your nerve. So, she was home and I had to duck into a closet for hours until she went to sleep and I could creep out and steal the book.

Creep out indeed.

I stared at her sleeping face and I watched her chest rise up and down. I started to feel the formation of attachment to her. She was beautiful to me, and I wanted touch her hair, so I did. Then I did it again. Then I ran my fingers through her hair one too many times and she stirred in her sleep. I almost dropped the book in panic. If I ever am discovered by humanity, getting caught molesting a sleeping woman's hair is not the first impression I want to make. I took the book and left, never went back. Not that I had the chance to. A few years later, that woman and her fat-headed husband died in a car wreck.

I was saddened to read that.

I do a lot of breaking into houses. Estate sales are a blessing and a curse. They are what I call a twofer. You get to scavenge things you need to live successfully on the outsides of society as a monster, plus estate sales usually follow deaths so I get to search for ghosts while I am at it. Usually one or the other presents itself. I also usually find things that I can sell online. Got to keep that rating up. Estate sales are a blessing. Love them.

But I hate death. Hate it. Don't know how you can just sit there and enjoy life knowing that for almost all of eternity, you won't exist, not as you are. Not as you know yourself today, and once you lose that, what are you? The day will come when no one you love will exist because of death. The planet Earth is spinning alone in infinity and one day even the planet will be gone. Just gone. I don't understand how you can fall sleep at night without staying awake thinking that you might not wake up. That some invisible physical defect deep in your brain could fail, flood your skull with blood and kill you. How do you not go insane?

Faith, maybe? I don't have that luxury. I know that SOMETHING happens to humans after they die. I've heard dead men talk. I've met demons. But what happens to me after I die?

Took me a few years before I put together enough experience and stability to be able to look past my own survival and start asking some deeper questions. Questions like, what am I and how do I get to keep being it? It's heavy stuff. Imagine not knowing if stubbing your toe is gonna shut your lights out forever. The first time I stepped out of my basement I thought

I was gonna die the second I crossed the threshold. Like, maybe the house itself was keeping me alive. I lived in fear constantly. *Live* in fear constantly. I'm honestly not much better off today.

What progress I've made is due to a book I scrounged, a book about the supernatural and the afterlife. I found a book that spoke of ghosts. And then I started stealing and reading anything I could on the paranormal, supernatural and spiritual. This was before the internet, by a long stretch. Now any palooka can hit up the dark web and find someone willing to sell spells and secrets and weak arcane items. My first spell book I had to get the old-fashioned way - I stole it from a witch. After I had killed her magician boyfriend. It was a crazy time.

Anyone involved in the mystical game will tell you, one spell leads to another. I started with some simple protection stuff. I cast one around Barris' abandoned house, one that strongly encouraged people to not see the house very well, and to forget about it once they've moved on. Less successful were the spells I cast on myself. I think it's because a house is a pretty common place, even an abandoned one in the woods, and editing it out of people's mind is pretty easy. A sentient automaton slinking about town is a bit more noticeable and harder to distract from. Yes, I started small but you can only know you have the ability to summon a demon for so long before you have to try it. In my case, I got through about 5 years before I called up my first. To say I was not prepared would be an understatement. I learned nothing, except to keep salt and rat blood on hand at all times.

Demons, as they are wont to do, lead to angels. Which, you learn quickly, cannot be summoned. I've never seen an angel. Never seen any sort of direct confirmation of any religion, by the way. I heard that the thing about vampires and crosses are true, although I've never actually seen a vampire myself, so I can't confirm that.

Then came the ghosts. Ghosts at least presented me with a direction. Ghosts are proof of the afterlife. Proof that somehow, there is a way to beat this horrible affliction of death. They give hope that everything we do, and everything we are, isn't for nothing. Have never understood why humans find the idea of ghosts so scary or repulsive or even silly. Wouldn't you welcome any evidence that you don't just blink out? Sometimes I wonder if I'm the only one taking this whole death thing seriously. We have to be more than this, don't we?

I say "we" but of course I am mostly aware that I am speaking about you. We don't yet know what I am, but I do know that I am here. I do know that

I am alive. Unlike the poor sad sack that I ripped from the Great Beyond to have a chat with. The ghost, let me finish telling you about the ghost.

I finished writing on my little chalkboard and looked back up at the ghost. He flinched when I caught his eye, and again when I extended my arm to show him what I had written. I wasn't worried he wouldn't understand it. I have excellent penmanship.

YOU'VE BEEN DEAD MANY YEARS. I HAVE BROUGHT YOU BACK TO TELL ME WHAT YOU SAW.

"No…" he said, shaking his head. I was taking a risk by telling him that. Finally being able to communicate with a ghost after a long dry spell may have made me a little, let's say, enthusiastic. If I shattered his mind, what use would he be? The last thing the world needs is yet another insane ghost. I certainly had my fill of them by that point, but I didn't know how long I had him, and I feared I already saw his form wafting a bit.

"I'm sick…. I'm hallucinating…..Alba," he stammered.

In frustration I wiped the sleeve of my trench coat along the chalkboard, erasing everything except TELL ME WHAT YOU SAW.

I thrust it out at him again, this time slamming my hand against the chalkboard instead of grabbing at him. I wanted his full attention but, in retrospect, I should have been more conscious of how scary I can come off. Scarier than a ghost, even. Fury and loud noises rarely help, except when they *really* help.

"I didn't see anything. Please. I was in bed, and now I'm here. This looks like my home but it's not," he said. "Help me. Please help me." He looked at me, pleading for answers. Good luck, pal.

Another swipe of the chalkboard and I started writing again, but it was pointless. He had gone silent and when I looked up, he was…frozen. Frozen is the only word for it.

His arms, still solid, were crossed over his chest as if he were mimicking the position of his corpse in its coffin. His mouth was twisted open as far as it could go as if screaming, but not a sound came out of his maw. His eyes were wide open with terror, and they stared at my face while giving no indication that he was actually looking at me or seeing me. In the brief second I looked away, something had terrified and seized him. More questions, no answers.

My music box tinkled.

Then the room filled with the sound of the most terrified scream I had ever heard, but it did not come forth from the ghost. The entire room screamed, or so it seemed to me. It came from the walls and the floor. It blasted down from the ceiling. I could feel the metal in my body vibrate and I instinctively pulled my trench coat tightly shut to protect myself. The ghost, still frozen, began to rise from the floor as the scream went on and on. The ghost's eyes stayed locked forward, staring at nothing but the passing wall behind me as it rose.

When the windows began to crack I started to back toward the door. I kept my eyes on the ghost as it rose higher and higher, but my feet moved of their own accord. Self-preservation being my first instinct, you understand. By the time I had reached the door, the books had begun to drop from the shelves. A few at first, then a waterfall of paper. At least they didn't fly at me. A particularly nasty poltergeist did that to me back in 1966 and the spine of a bible dinged my forehead. The ding is still there. I sometimes find myself playing with it when I am thinking.

The scream continued. I dropped my chalkboard and didn't or couldn't even hear it clatter to the floor. This unnaturally loud, long scream. No throat of flesh and blood could produce this and maintain it. The vocal cords would shred. No, this *sounded* human, but the very air was screaming. The house itself, maybe.

Then the ghost's eyes were upon me. They didn't move, mind you. One moment they were staring straight ahead and the next, they glared down at me. Like a film frame had been snipped out of existence. The expression of them changed as well. Confusion had fled and fear had taken root in that ghost's eyes. I know fear, trust in that. I was very afraid in that room, to be clear. I'm not a hard case at all. If I could speak I think I would have screamed as well. I think I would have babbled out an apology. To the ghost for bringing it here. To whatever was screaming. I wanted to beg it to stop before I lost whatever my mind is.

My back hit the door and the scream stopped, cut off as if someone had flipped a switch. I looked at the ghost and saw that it had become incorporate again. It still hovered near the ceiling, and those fearful eyes still looked down on me, but now as misty as any ghost I had seen before. The spell was broken.

So I thought.

The ghost snapped its mouth open and shut a few times.

"You don't know what you've done," he said. "It sees me now."

Then, the ghost shot through the ceiling and disappeared from my sight. I stared for a moment, then ran from the room and up the steps toward the second floor, the metal trestle of my legs squealing against the formed brass that makes up what counts as my skin. Normally even that slight proof of internal friction would cause me to slow down, but not on this night. I can move with haste when I need to, and I dashed past pictures of the happy family that lived in this house. Did I mention I had broken into this house, after weeks of watching and waiting for the perfect night to sneak in to do this? Seems like the sort of detail that's easy to lose when writing about this sort of stuff.

Annoyingly, there was nothing upstairs. No sign of the unlucky phantom. No destruction to rival the room downstairs and, thankfully, no screaming. I don't think I could have taken any more of that scream. I waited around a bit. I even tried to summon the ghost again, but this time there was no connection. Nothing remained of it within the walls, I could tell. There is a feeling you get inside of a haunted house. You know what it is, I think. You've no doubt felt it and despite talking yourself out of it, you were most likely right.

The ghost was gone. I felt vaguely guilty about that, but it's not like I actually know what happened to it. It's equally plausible that despite its obvious distress, I could have been the thing that propelled that man's spirit onward to its final heavenly destination, back into the arms of his beloved Alba. Sure, I admit it didn't exactly seem that way in the moment, but again, some things are my problem and some things aren't. Since there was no way to know, and since I had made it out the other end with no damage to myself, I'll consider this a win. Moral ambiguity is something that I do indeed have the luxury of maintaining in instances such as these.

It was time to leave, so I checked the street through the small window on the front door of the house. It was still late, or early, I guess. Between three and four in the morning. There was no one out on the street. No cop cars coming to investigate a horrifying scream heard in the night by a do-good neighbor, so I tightened the trench coat around me and pulled my fedora as far down over my face as I could and slipped out of the house.

It saw me, he said. I had that to ponder as I made my way back home. It lifted my spirits as it stoked my fear. *Something* is out there. Something I didn't know about yesterday. Something that looks upon the dead if they aren't careful. Good or bad, that something that may be able to give me the answers to my mystery. I shrugged deeper into my trench coat, as if to stave off the cold air that didn't really bother me. Why should it? I'm alive and I'm on the case.

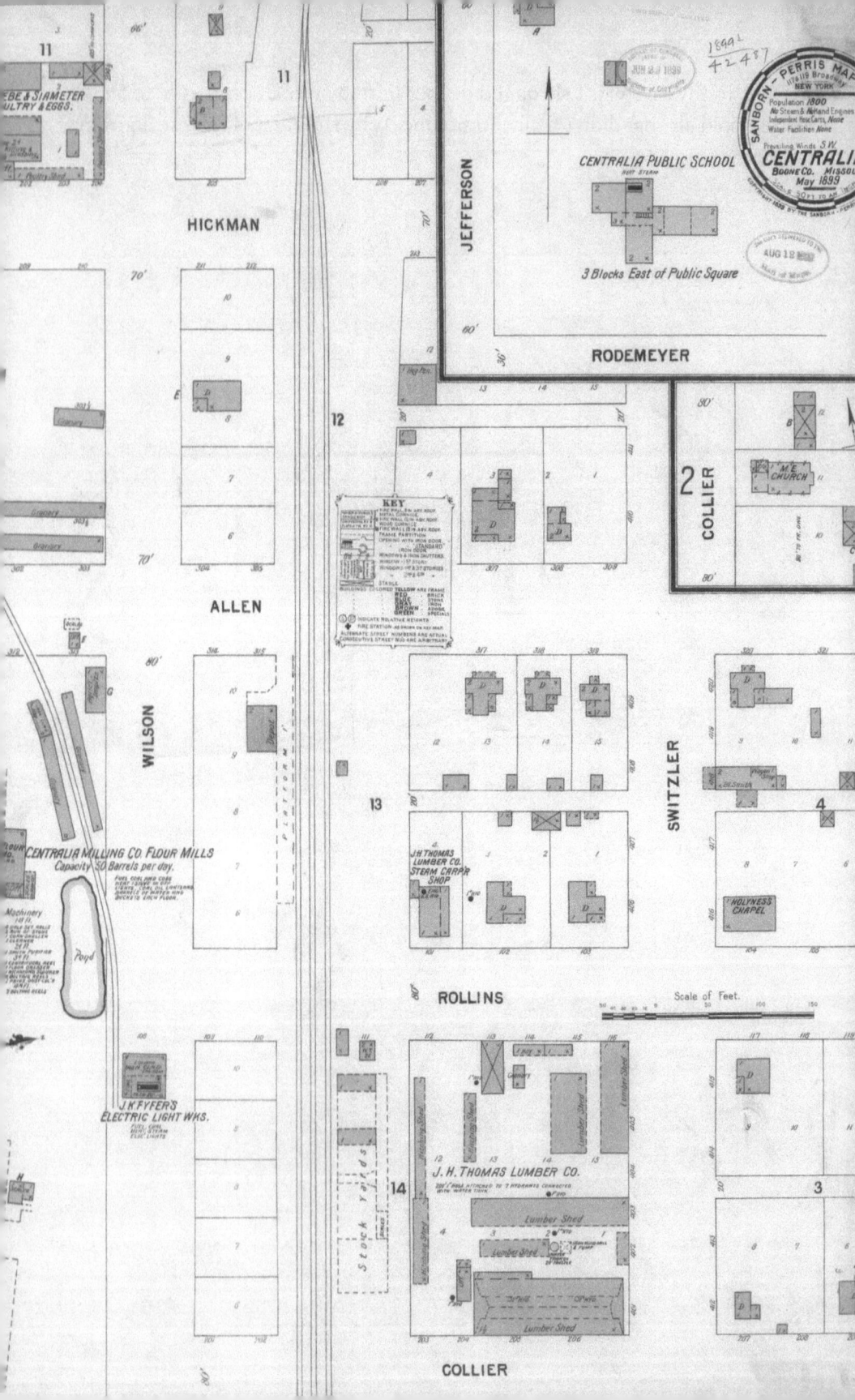

SANBORN - PERRIS MAP
114-119 Broadway
NEW YORK

Population 1800
No Steam & Hand Engines
Independent Hose Carts, None
Water Facilities None

Prevailing Winds S.W.
CENTRALIA
BOONE CO.   MISSOURI
May 1899

1899
42487

CENTRALIA PUBLIC SCHOOL

3 Blocks East of Public Square

HICKMAN

JEFFERSON

RODEMEYER

COLLIER

2

M.E. CHURCH

KEY

12

ALLEN

WILSON

13

CENTRALIA MILLING CO. FLOUR MILLS
Capacity 50 Barrels per day.

J.H. THOMAS
LUMBER CO.
STEAM CARP'R.
SHOP

SWITZLER

4

HOLYNESS
CHAPEL

Pond

J.K. FYFER'S
ELECTRIC LIGHT WKS.

ROLLINS

Scale of Feet.

14

Stock Yards

J.H. THOMAS LUMBER CO.

Lumber Shed

Lumber Shed

Lumber Shed

3

COLLIER

The Grasp of Wraiths

Cullen Bunn

Centralia, MO

Location of Centralia, Missouri
Coordinates: 39°12′35″N 92°8′11″W
Country   United States
State   Missouri
Counties   Audrain, Boone
Area
 • Total   2.86 sq mi (7.40 km2)
Population
 • Total   4,027
First Epicenter Sighting
 • January 1974
Percent Burn
 • 52%

I don't work well with others, at least not if they're alive.

The living come with too much baggage. Ambition. Grief. Jealousy. Agendas. Successes. Failures. They have too much to lose. Makes them untrustworthy. The dead, on the other hand, have nothing to prove, no reason to lie. They've already lost everything.

Or so they think.

I know better.

I've gone by many titles over the years, most of them hated by the living and the dead alike. Sorcerer, warlock, thaumaturge, charlatan, trickster, heathen. All accurate to some degree—the same degree, in fact, to which they are inaccurate.

These days I prefer "necromancer," though that's not exactly right on the money, either.

More palatable, maybe, than the truth.

And work is work.

***

I had been on the road for nearly twelve hours when I passed my first horse-drawn buggy. A couple of bearded men sat in the driver's seat, shaded from the mid-morning sun. They glanced toward the Tahoe as I veered around and accelerated. Their scowls, spied in the side view mirror, were closer than they appeared.

The blacktop followed rolling hills past fields and fence posts, red barns and farmhouses. On one side of the road, acres of crops, long past harvest, stretched into the distance. On the other side, a few gnarled, leafless trees, bare for the approach of winter, stood sentinel along the shoulder. Beyond the twisted trees, a few more farms slowly rotted into obscurity. And beyond the dying farms, a thick forest of evergreens grew wild.

A yellow caution sign warned me to "share the road" with both horse and cart.

Amish country.

A testimony to simpler times.

My SUV, on the other hand, was testimony to interstate fast food, truck stops, and No-Doz. Candy wrappers and empty soda bottles and greasy, crumpled fast food bags littered the passenger seat and floorboard. I had been living on the road for longer than I cared to consider, moving from motel to motel, sometimes catching a little sleep at rest areas, not bothering with many carwashes. The Tahoe was relatively new—less than a year old—but the lifestyle was not. I had run my previous vehicle ragged, until the only things holding it together were gravity, friction, and faith. I couldn't afford to get stranded in one place for too long, so it had been time to trade up. But I was doing my best to replace the Tahoe's new car smell with the "lived in" patina of my old vehicle.

Another horse-drawn buggy slipped into view as I crested a hill, gliding past, then vanishing from the rear view. The horse was white. The driver's face was solemn, shrouded in shadow, but his lips moved, his mouth forming an endless stream of words I could not hear. I watched the driver and buggy in the mirror, watched as they grew smaller and smaller and then vanished behind the hills. The entire time the driver spoke, as if determined to deliver a message I couldn't hear or understand.

Maybe he was praying to ward off foul presences.

Maybe he was cursing his lot in life.

Maybe he was singing a Foghat tune. Foghat. That's what the Amish liked, right?

Or maybe he was welcoming me to Centralia, Missouri.

Welcoming or warning.

Either way worked.

***

All things considered, Centralia was a fine town. Nothing wrong with it, really. Situated almost in the middle of a state that's almost in the middle of the country. A community of farms and emerging businesses, of summer festivals and picnics, of churches old and new, of tractor parades and civil war reenactments. Friends and neighbors knew one another, helped one another, and cared about one another.

No wonder I didn't like the place.

I preferred a little less community in my communities.

Healthy doses of skepticism and disassociation and isolation and—yes—even paranoia formed the foundation of my day-to-day interactions and indeed my survival. I had picked it up from the dead, I suppose. Believe me, if they had their druthers, they wouldn't allow their mortal remains to be buried so close to one another for all eternity. The anti-social attitudes of the dearly departed had served me well and kept me alive on more than one occasion.

I'd been through the area before. More than once, actually. It had been long ago, though, and I barely remembered it. No one in town would remember— or recognize—me. That suited me just fine. If ever someone living, dead, or in between looked at me with even a vague sense of remembrance, the harbingers of disaster started shrieking in my ears. I shouldn't be remembered, not fondly nor with spite. If I was smart, I'd never be more than a shadow, almost a ghost myself, slipping from one place to the next, never making an impression.

But I wasn't all that smart.

I was here because someone—a friend—remembered me.

A friend.

Not really. More like an old rival. An enemy even.

But close enough.

She didn't know the truth about me, but she knew enough to ask me to help her with the murderous ghosts that were plaguing the town.

***

Like a vulture, I circled the streets of Centralia a time or three, taking in the sights, getting a feel for my surroundings. The town had changed a great deal since my last visit. Now, there was a McDonalds and a Sonic and a Dollar Tree. Now, there were gift boutiques and pawn shops and car dealerships.

Up ahead, a railroad signal flashed, and a crossing gate lowered slowly. I pulled to a stop, letting the SUV idle before the gate. For a moment, I saw no train, heard no train. The signal bell clanged a promise that had yet to be fulfilled. Could the signal and gate be malfunctioning? I amused myself with the idea that a ghost train—unseen but there just the same—rocketed down the tracks.

Soon enough, I heard a blaring horn, and a train—a real, land-of-the-living train—thundered past, a line of hoppers and boxcars rumbling along the tracks, moving fast as if making up for lost time. I felt vibrations shuddering up through the tires of the Tahoe, through the floorboard. The signal post shimmied a little as the red lights bounced from one side to the other.

I remembered the railroad.

Of course, I did.

I remembered the screams.

After the train passed, I pulled across the tracks and drove further into town. I found the diner—Gently's Family Dining—where my old rival had wanted to meet, and I parked alongside the curb. I still had time to kill, but I had grown weary of the SUV and its trash floormats, weary of driving. I hopped out, stretched, letting my back crack loudly. A stroll, I thought, might do me good, might remind my legs how to work on their own.

Across the street, I saw another horse and buggy, parked next to cars and pickups, just outside a small gift boutique. "Amish Crafts and Gifts," read the sign in the window. I crossed the street and approached the horse that was hitched to the wagon.

The animal snorted and stomped.

Uneasy.

It sensed my presence.

And it didn't like it.

The horse's nervousness was infectious. I felt a wave of uncertainty and paranoia. Fear. I felt as if I was being watched. I looked around, turning slowly in place, but saw nothing out of the ordinary.

That wasn't good enough.

Reaching into my inside jacket pocket, I withdrew a small vial. I held it between my thumb and forefinger, moving it slowly back and forth, letting the glass catch the light. To the average person, the vial might appear empty, but I saw a curl of ethereal vapor within. It glowed softly, churning, writhing, pressing against the walls of the container. I watched for a moment, almost mesmerized by the undulating presence.

"What's that?"

The voice pulled my attention away from the phylactery. I closed my hand around the vial and turned.

A little boy stood before me. He was maybe six years old, with dark hair and dark eyes. He wore a plain white shirt, suspenders, black pants, and a broad-brimmed straw hat. Amish, by the looks of him.

"What's that you're staring at?" he asked again.

"Oh, nothing." I closed my hand around the vial. "A canary in a coal mine."

"A coal mine?"

"Just an expression."

"No coal mines here that I know about." His face told me he was putting a lot of thought toward the subject. "I dream about one sometimes, though. An old one. Burning."

I cocked my head and regarded the child. There was something about him. An unseen aura. A power. I reached out and opened my hand, presenting the vial to the boy. He shuffle-stepped closer and craned his neck for a better look.

"What do you see?" I asked.

"There's something moving inside," he said, "and, whatever it is, it... glows."

"Do you know what it is?"

He looked up at me, but before he could answer, his father called for him.

"Isaiah, come away now. Leave that man alone."

The boy's father was tall and lean, dressed in dark clothing, wearing a straw hat similar to his son's. He sported a dark beard. He stood in the door of the boutique, beckoning for the boy.

"It's all right," I said. "He wasn't bothering me."

Isaiah took one last look at the phylactery, then glanced up at me, shrugged, and hurried to his father's side. The boy slipped past his father and into the gift shop. The father watched me—coldly—for a moment, then stepped back into the shadows, letting the door swing shut.

"I see you still have a knack for making friends."

Tucking the phylactery back into my pocket, I turned to greet the speaker.

"Just becoming acquainted with the locals while waiting for you," I said. "You're late."

"You're early, Alex, which is... not like you."

I hadn't seen Cayce Rainer in a few years, but she was still wearing the same faded black denim jacket. The jacket was well-worn, threadbare and frayed in places, but the rest of her ensemble—the simple maroon top, the deep black leggings, the boots—somehow managed to class it up. Her brown hair was cut short on the sides and back, her bangs so long that she constantly, without thinking about it, had to brush it away from her dark eyes. She smirked, an expression that seemed as ever-present with her as the jacket, as she regarded me.

"You look well," I said.

"You look the same," she said.

"I don't like change."

"Let me buy you a cup of coffee."

***

Only a handful of people have my direct line. Most potential clients can only reach me through Mortimer "the Mortician" Morris—agent to the necromancers. I'd been working with Mort since before he called himself Mort. In his youth, which had faded long ago despite the rich blackness of his regularly dyed hair, he had actually been a mortician. But once he startled peeling back the layers of the realm of occult spiritualism and mysticism, he realized he could make a better living as a manager for sorcerous types. He kept my schedule clean and organized, made sure I wasn't bothered with requests to commune with dead pets and the like. Mort was worth his weight in gold, and he rarely let me forget it. Occasionally, though, old acquaintances reached out directly and asked for consultations or assistance.

Mort, of course, hated such calls with the fiery passion of a man who was being denied his commission.

Not that he had much say in the matter.

Cayce knew how to contact me without the middleman, though she rarely capitalized on said knowledge. As she wove her way through the diner's breakfast crowd, I tried to recall how long it had been since I'd seen her. Five years, maybe more. It had been a case of possession, that much I remembered. Not demonic possession. Neither one of us played around with demons if we could help it. A dead man's restless spirit had tried to take up residence in the flesh and blood of his grandson. The kid barely survived the experience.

Sometimes, the dead can be real dicks.

We took one of the few remaining tables in Gently's, sat silently across from one another as the waitress used a warm, wet rag to wipe away crumbs and maple syrup residue, and remained silent for a few minutes more after she hurried away with our orders. We had plenty to say to each other, but we weren't saying it yet.

I became acutely aware of other eyes on us. The other patrons—men and women from every walk of Centralia life—stared in our direction as they chewed their bacon and sipped their coffee. They all shared the same baggy-eyed look of weariness and unease. They were haunted, these people. They might have been trying to keep their lives moving predictably forward to their inevitable ending, but something was keeping them up at night, filling them with dread. Their stares were helpless, pleading.

After a few seconds—and after the waitress had brought our coffee—I asked Cayce, "Why am I here?"

She poured an ungodly amount of sugar and creamer into her cup. "I thought we were old friends."

"That's a bit of a stretch, don't you think? The last time we saw each other, you threatened to stab me in the eye with a spirit board planchette."

"That's not true."

"No?"

"It wasn't your eye."

"Funny how the passing of time makes memories sweeter."

A man—thin and tall and sallow, with sunken eyes and greasy dark hair—pulled away from the gawkers and shuffled toward us. A fine sheen of sweat covered his pale skin, soaked through his t-shirt around the collar and under his arms. He approached the table, staring right at me the entire time. I'm not sure he blinked.

"Who's this?" He asked. He stood close, his legs pressed against the table's edge.

Cayce sighed. "Hello, Abram."

"Is he like you?" Abram never took his eyes off me. "Is he another ghost-killer?"

"You can't kill ghosts," I said. It was a lie, but I didn't think a guy like Abram would understand such things. "They're already dead. I'm an... associate of Ms. Rainer. We were just discussing this town's spiritual crisis. If you'll excuse us—"

"I offered to help," Abram said. "I told her I'd be willing to help her with these ghosts. Maybe if she'd accepted my help, she wouldn't need you."

"Abram—" Cayce's voice grew stern. "—I've already told you. You're not trained for something like this, not prepared. You don't understand what we're dealing with. If you did, you wouldn't have asked for what you did."

Abram shifted his dark eyes away from me and toward Cayce. He chewed upon the inside of his mouth, like he wanted to tell her something, but didn't dare. Then he looked back at me.

"She could have spared you from what's coming."

And with that, he shuffled away.

"He seems nice," I said.

"Alex, I'm in a fix here." Cayce took a breath, steeling herself for a bit of self-awareness. "I admit, I thought I was looking at easy money. Come into town, exorcise a few errant spirits, be on my way to the next job before most of the locals even knew I was here. But it's not that simple. Whatever's manifesting here, it's angry and it's mean, and that makes it powerful."

There was something in her eyes, something I hadn't seen from her before, not even when we'd been in the thick of it.

"You're scared."

"Don't enjoy this too much."

"Sorry. It's just that I've never seen you rattled like this. Whatever you've stumbled into—"

"There's something about this job. There's something about this place. It feels… wrong."

I knew better than to brush aside her "feelings" too readily.

"Will you help me?" she asked.

"Why don't you introduce me to these manifestations of yours?"

"Don't worry," she said. "You'll meet them."

"That sounds ominous."

"You have no idea."

***

But I did.

Quaint or not, Centralia, Missouri was the site of one of the bloodiest massacres of the Civil War.

On September 27, 1864, pro-Confederate William "Bloody Bill" Anderson and 80 guerrillas arrived in Centralia with designs on cutting off the North Missouri Railroad. Wearing stolen Union Army uniforms, Anderson's men ransacked and looted the town. They hooted and yowled and sang songs of death and glory while they fueled their bloodlust by drinking whiskey from their stolen Union boots.

They toasted the reapers without even realizing it.

Anderson blocked the rail line, stopping an approaching train, and his men poured on board like common bandits. They dragged the frightened passengers from the train, finding—to their mash-fueled delight—two dozen Union soldiers among the civilians. The soldiers were unarmed, on leave after the Battle of Atlanta, and heading home to visit with their families. But that didn't matter to Bloody Bill.

Desperate prayers, like rotting meat for the flies.

The Union prisoners were ordered at gunpoint to strip out of their uniforms. When Anderson called for an officer to step forward, a young Sergeant stepped up, fully expecting to be killed while the others were spared. But the guerrillas took the sergeant captive while they commenced to shooting the others.

Like sacrifices.

Not satisfied with killing their enemies, they scalped them. They cut open their bellies with bayonets and stuff their bodies with the bones of cattle.

No wonder the reapers started thinking of themselves as gods.

They set fire to the train and the depot, then rode out of town, howling with cruel laughter along the way.

The smoke took the shape of black-winged angels.

Later that day, a regiment of Union soldiers arrived in Centralia. Aghast at the mutilation of their fellow blues, they set out in pursuit of the guerrillas. They encountered them not far from town. They outnumbered Anderson's men, and the Union commander—Major Johnston—ordered his forces to dismount and form a line, ready to meet their enemies in a stand-up fight.

More offerings.

Anderson's men rode right over them, blasting at them with revolvers while the Union soldiers fired a startled volley and struggled to reload their Enfield rifles. Almost all of the Union soldiers—including Major Johnston—died.

The psychopomps were busy that day.

So, yeah, I had some idea what Cayce had called me to help her with.

Or so I thought.

Knowing everything I knew, I should have expected when everything got much, much worse.

***

Cayce recited the story of the Centralia Massacre, and I listened and nodded as if it was the first time I'd heard the tale. She had some of her facts wrong, but I didn't correct her. She would've hated that. And she reminded me that the infamous Jesse James had been one of the murderous guerrillas under Bloody Bill's command.

"A town like this," she said, "with its history, of course there are ghost stories."

"But not like this."

"Not at all."

We walked through town as we talked. The streets were lined with buildings, some of which might have stood at the time of the Massacre. Antique shops and gift stores and jewelry emporiums and diners now occupied every space. Massive trees, which might have also stood as sentinels or saplings during the slaughter, lined the streets and even rose between buildings, creating natural spots for small parks and alleys. A few citizens took note of us as we passed. In a town like Centralia, it probably didn't take long for rumors to spread. Many people knew that Cayce was here to help them with their "ghost problem." As a stranger in her company, I must have been regarded in the same light. Another ghost hunter.

Or "ghost-killer."

"That guy, back at the diner—"

"Abram."

"That's the one. What's his deal?"

"He's harmless enough, I guess. When I first got to town, he wanted to help me. But he wanted something in return. His sister died a couple of years ago. Pneumonia, I believe. He wanted me to bring her back."

I've always thought it was funny how people thought magicians could resurrect the dead. Not even the most powerful necromancers could do such a thing. We have some power over death, but none over life itself. Only one person has ever been able to pull off the resurrection trick, and He doesn't dedicate a lot of time to solving ghostly murders.

"He wasn't too happy when I turned him down," Cayce said.

"They never are."

"The mayor and chief of police hired me," Cayce said. "They did an internet search for 'paranormal investigation' and I popped up. They don't know anything about what I do. They don't even believe in it. But with people dying in such awful ways, I guess they got desperate."

"How many?" I asked.

"Six before I arrived. Three more since. Nine total."

As we walked along, a police cruiser glided up alongside the curb. The driver—a fresh-faced officer—unrolled the window and called out to us.

"Ms. Rainer," the officer said, "you're going to want to come with me. There's been another one."

As we climbed into the cruiser—Cayce in the front, me in the back—she looked at me across the vehicle's roof.

"Make that ten," she said.

***

I'd tell you it was the first time I'd taken a ride in the back of a cop car, but I'd be lying. And, really, you'll find I lie more than I should. Sometimes it grows old, even for me. This ride was more comfortable than the other six. At least I wasn't handcuffed.

After ten minutes, the officer pulled over in a small residential area. All the houses looked the same—small, white, carports off to the side, surrounded by trees and overgrown lawns. Good starter homes for young couples... or ending places for the elderly. Four other police cars—I'm guessing the town's complete complement—were parked along the street. None of the lights were flashing. A small group of dour-faced cops gathered in the yard of one of the houses, their shoulders slumped, their faces pale and haunted. The front door of the house stood open, and I saw figures moving around inside as we approached.

I smelled blood ten paces from the front steps.

It grew stronger.

"What's happening here?" I asked Cayce as we drew closer.

"It's like I told you," she said. "I've never seen anything like it."

"Can you smell that?"

"Smell what?"

"Are you certain we're dealing with ghosts?"

"I've seen them."

Inside, the smell of decay would have overwhelmed the senses of nearly anyone else. Cayce put a hand over her nose and mouth, like she was going to throw up. The smell of death never bothered me, though. I'd been breathing it so long, I barely noticed it.

The blood, though...

The stink of it was almost unbearable here. Not just blood, I realized. There was that, yes, but something else assaulted my senses, something only someone like me can smell.

Dead blood.

There's a difference.

Blood is spilled from the living. It's bright and hot and red and smells of copper. Dead blood comes from the unliving, and it is cold and dark and smells like rot. Not every ghost oozes with the stuff. Only those who died horrible, violent deaths; only those who shrieked in horror and agony while their living blood poured from their flesh; only those who couldn't forget, even in death, what had been done to them in their final moments.

Wraiths.

Please don't let it be wraiths, I thought.

Because no one gets out of an encounter with wraiths unscathed.

As we entered the house, the chief of police stepped out into the front hallway to meet us. He was a tall man, broad-shouldered, and stern. He was red-faced. I wasn't sure if that was the usual state of being for him, or if whatever he had seen in the house had brought on the reaction. He stomped toward us, fingers hitching his belt, and eyed me coldly.

"Who the hell is this?"

"This is Alex Crawford," Cayce said, "an associate of mine. He has some expertise in matters like these. I thought he might be able to help."

"Expertise." The chief almost spat the word from his mouth. "We'll see about that, won't we? Come on. The body's in the kitchen."

He turned and stomped deeper into the house. We followed.

Not wraiths, I silently pleaded.

But when I saw the body of their latest victim, I knew my hopes had been dashed.

The mutilated man sat at a small table in the middle of a small kitchen. He wore the grease-stained coveralls of a mechanic. From the looks of it, he had come home from work and poured himself a bowl of sugary cereal. But he never got to take a bite.

The spoon was still in his rigid fingers.

The colorful loops had gone soggy in bloody milk.

He sagged in his seat, his eyes open, his head down, his mouth hanging agape. The front of his coveralls had been ripped open, as was his chest. His skin was shredded and peeled away, his ribs cracked and pulled open like cabinet doors. He had been hollowed, his organs clawed out and messily spread across the tabletop. In place of his stomach, lungs and heart, rotting, inhuman bones had been shoved into the orifice. A ring of gore spattered the floor around his chair.

The blood of the living.

But the inhuman bones dripped with the bilious, stinking blood of the dead.

"His name's Gary Finch," the chief said. "Works at Jenner's Body Shop. Worked, I mean. He missed his shift, didn't call in, didn't answer his phone, so his boss came to check on him. He was a good guy. Drank a little too much on a Saturday night, maybe, but he never crossed anybody that I know of, never got into any trouble. He damn sure didn't deserve this."

"You said you saw them." I turned to Cayce, dropped my voice low. "The ghosts. What did they look like?"

She struggled to pull her gaze away from the murder scene. "They were beings of light, bobbing slowly in the shadows, near one of the murder scenes, not long after I arrived. There were three of them. I tried to banish them, and I thought at first that it worked."

"Well it didn't," the chief said.

"I know," Cayce said, then spoke to me once more. "They vanished from my sight on that night. It was like they were watching me, and when I worked the incantation, they simply vanished. I haven't seen them since, but they keep killing people."

No, I thought, *no being of light did this.*

If wraiths were plaguing Centralia, it was no wonder Cayce hadn't been able to help. If ghosts were little sprinkles of the afterlife, wraiths were torrential downpours. They were fueled by anguish and torment and hatred stronger than death. Wraiths, though, didn't tend to linger. They weren't the type for long-lasting hauntings. They were not intelligent. Their own anguish and torment devoured any last vestiges of intelligence. On the rare occasion they spilled into this world, they burned out fast.

And they did a lot of damage while they were here.

"If you don't mind," I said. "I'd like a minute alone with the body."

Cayce hesitated. A question waited on her lips. Instead, she looked at the chief and nodded in agreement. The chief eyed me, hooked his fingers through his belt loops to pull up his pants, then issued a curt order to clear the room. Cayce, the chief, and the officers shuffled out, leaving me alone with the body.

I looked at the corpse. The stillness, the quiet, comforted me. Even in my line of work—especially in my line of work—I preferred when the deceased had nothing to say.

But I knew it couldn't last.

"What do you have to say for yourself?" I asked.

Only, I didn't speak any human language. I didn't utter a word that any other living creature could possibly understand.

The language of the dead is only for the dead.

And when I spoke it, the dead listened.

The corpse bucked in the chair, almost as if a shock had passed through the cold flesh. The fingers contracted, the nails scraping at the metal beneath them. The mouth twitched open.

Flesh likes to hold onto the spirit for as long as it can.

"Where—?"

The unspoken voice materialized first, followed by the apparition. The mechanic's ghost flickered into view, almost like the glow of a guttering lightbulb struggling to stay lit. He looked pale and weak, and the numerous slices covered his body, only now the blood of the unliving gushed from the wounds in sheets, down his neck and chest and arms and legs, pooling on the floor beneath him.

"Where am I?" He asked.

"Take a look around," I said. *"I think you already know."*

He looked toward the corpse, as if his vision was just now clearing, as if he was only now seeing his own body.

"Try to stay calm," I said. *"Out-of-body experiences can be traumatic, especially permanent ones like yours. But if you panic, you might attract unwanted attention. There are hungry little beasts out there in the ether. No sense in chumming the waters."*

"I'm dead?"

"That's what I want to talk about."

"I... don't want to be dead."

"I'm afraid that's not your call, friend."

"Are you dead, too?"

I shook my head.

"Then how is it that I'm talking to you?"

"I guess you're just lucky."

"Can you help me?"

"That's not how this works. I conjured you up so you could help me. And you can start by telling me exactly how you died."

***

I stepped out of the house, thinking to myself that I'd be better off blowing town and forgetting any reward for ridding them of their wraiths. The chief, Cayce, and a small gathering of police milled around the front yard.

"Want to tell me what that was all that about?" The chief growled.

"I'm here to help," I said.

"I've heard that before." The chief cast a cold look in Cayce's direction. "But I've still got another dead body to deal with, don't I?"

"You'll have more if you keep slowing me down with questions, especially when you couldn't possibly wrap your head around the answers if I gave them to you."

"What did you—"

"These aren't phantoms in white sheets, chief. These aren't goblins that pop out from behind bushes and shout 'boo!' The entities you're dealing with are old and powerful. And they're angry. That anger of theirs is so strong, they can actually touch this world. When they do that, they only grow more angry. The angrier they get, the stronger they get, a vicious little circle. If you don't let Cayce and me handle this now, they'll be so powerful that no one will be able to stop them."

The chief chewed on the inside of his cheek.

"All right, Mr. Crawford. How are you and Ms. Rainer planning on 'handling' our little problem?"

"We'll start," I said, "with the train."

***

We waited.

I picked a stretch of railroad just outside of town, secluded from the buildings and crossing gates and streetlights, a barren expanse of dried grass giving rise to a slight hill. Atop the hill, surrounded by white stones, lined with metal, girded in timber, the rail sliced across the countryside.

Silent.

Still.

Waiting, just like us.

I had parked my Tahoe in the grass, finally putting its off-road capabilities to work in the most pitiful way possible. I left the engine running, the headlights flaring, the exhaust pluming into the air. I stood outside, though, leaning against the front grill, feeling the warmth of the engine. Cayce paced nearby, growing more impatient with every step.

"Don't you think I've thought of this?" she asked. "I'm not new to the game."

Compared to me, you are.

"The massacre," she said, "was the first thing I considered. All of those soldiers, pulled off the train, mutilated and murdered. Something like that is a breeding ground for ghosts. There's bound to be some sort of long-lasting resonance."

"A breeding ground for ghosts," I chuckled. "A bit dramatic, but I like it. A ghost orgy. All these specters and apparitions, fucking their brains out, giving birth to mean little ghost babies."

"Don't be crude."

"Have we met?"

"You know what I mean." She crossed her arms angrily. Her eyes narrowed. "Must you always be so damn superior?"

I watched the rail.

"Anyway," Cayce said, "you can sit out here all night and never experience—"

A train whistle, deep and lonely, howled in the darkness.

Not wanting to prove Cayce's point about superiority, I tried not to smile.

"You've got to be kidding me," Cayce muttered.

The whistle bellowed.

A ghostly cry.

"What did you do?" Cayce asked.

I pulled myself away from the car, took a few steps closer to the rail. "If anyone and everyone could see every ghost train that blasted along the tracks, they'd be looking at an almost endless stream of rotting, crumbling boxcars, passenger cars overfilled with restless spirits, engines spewing apparitions instead of steam and smoke. Country music and the dead; they're both drawn to trains. They're always running, but we can't usually see or hear them."

"You conjured it into the physical world."

"You brought me out here for a reason."

Now, we could hear the train—the whistle, yes, but also the hiss of steam, the rattle of the boxcars, the shriek of the wheels on the tracks, the chugging thunder of the engine. In the distance, a pale circle of light appeared. The soft glow of ghostly smoke, churning in the air, taking phantom shapes, then breaking apart. The train itself, wreathed in an otherworldly vapor.

Cayce watched in horror.

"Whatever spills out of that train—"

"I can handle it," I said.

At least, I hope so.

Cold wind—far colder than it should be—buffeted against us as the train slowed to a stop, the brakes hissing and screeching. Puffs of steam rose and fell from under the ghost train, the shapes of hideous ghosts rising, as if trying to claw their way up from below, then collapsing and vanishing.

I reached into my pocket, wrapped my hand around the phylactery.

I could feel the energy within the glass vial, flickering, shivering.

Nothing emerged from the train, but through the windows of the passenger cars I saw shadowy shapes, sitting in the seats, still, veiled in mists and cobwebs, waiting, forever waiting, in hopes that the next stop would be the last.

But trains aren't psychopomps.

And the ghosts on board would likely ride those rails forever.

The soldiers materialized before us.

"Oh, God," Cayce gasped.

She knew. She understood what she was looking at.

Wraiths.

They were hunched, butchered, shambling shadows. They had all been scalped, their blood-slicked skulls gleaming, hairy flaps of skin hanging down in tatters over the backs of their necks or in front of their faces. Their bodies had been viciously ripped open, and bones had been shoved into the ragged and bleeding cavities. The bones were large—the remains of cattle—and gnawed upon but still covered in bits of dark and veiny meat. Carcasses stuffed with carcasses. As the figures staggered along, jerking and spasming, the bones churned like broken gears, scraping together.

They lurched toward me, their fingers twitching, ready to rip into my flesh.

Ready to tear my organs out.

Ready to stuff me full of charnel bones.

"Stop."

I spoke the language of the dead.

And the wraiths shambled to a halt. They stood there stupidly, staring at me with their empty eyes, their mouths hanging open. A few cattle bones fell to the ground at their feet.

The bones dripped oily blood.

"You're done here," I said in words only the dead could understand. *"Here in Centralia, here on this plane."*

I looked toward the ghost train. I willed it to move on, and it started chugging ahead once more. Lethargically. Reluctantly. The train knew it was leaving something behind. But it also knew that it could not disobey.

The train knew who the fuck it was dealing with.

The wraiths watched me coldly. They knew who I was, too. They wanted to murder me because of that knowledge.

"I didn't abandon you," I said. *"I didn't cast you into the In-Between. I understand if you don't believe me. I understand if you look at me and see those who tossed you aside. But I also know that after a while, Purgatory can feel a lot like Hell. And, if you'll let me... if you'll hear me out... I'll set things right."*

Cayce's breath caught in her throat. She panted, as if she had suddenly been dunked in a lake of ice water. Her eyes were going bloodshot. They might very well bleed before I was done.

"Wh-what are you saying?" She asked.

I ignored her.

I spoke to the wraiths once more, using the words only they could understand.

"Go."

And they started fading out of sight, one by one, going out like snuffed flames.

All save one.

The wraith moved once more, spasming and twitching as it went, dripping ichor. It walked past me, walked past Cayce, ignoring us both.

"What are you doing?" Cayce asked. "Why wouldn't you banish them all? Why would you let even one slip by? If it kills someone—"

"Those wraiths killed people," I said, "but someone else was pulling their strings."

Someone else speaks the language of the dead.

"We'll leave the car here," I said.

And we followed the dead.

***

Like an obedient hound, the undead soldier led us away from town, deep into the woods. We followed through thick forests. We scrambled over fallen trees. We waded through ankle-deep streams. The wraith was relentless, never stopping. It knew where to take us. It knew what to show us.

When we came upon a rusting, sagging mobile home, I waved a hand, spoke a dead word, and dismissed the wraith, letting him dissipate into mist.

"What is this?" Cayce asked? "Where are we?"

"The end of the road," I said.

The mobile home was old. My guess is it had been hauled onto the lot when most of the trees—tall now—were just saplings. The roof sagged. The rusty walls looked ready to buckle. Someone lived here, though. There were lights glowing from within. A wash line was draped between the trees, and clothing—tee shirts and jeans—had yet to be taken down. A dirt track, not much more than a pair of tire tracks wearing streaks into the thick grass, stretched into the darkness. An old pickup truck, dripping oil into the dirt and grass, was parked out front.

"Do you know who lives here?" I asked Cayce, maybe a little more forcefully than I intended. My nerves were at surface level. My trust, however, had shriveled to a nearly non-existent tickle.

Cayce shook her head.

"Whoever it is," I said, "they've found a way to summon the dead, to command an unseen spirit train to stop, to unleash those wraiths upon this town."

"Another necromancer," Cayce said.

"I don't think so. We're dealing with a hammer here, not a surgical instrument. If it is a necromancer, they're unfocused, in the infancy of their powers. At the same time, though, they shouldn't be able to do the things they've done."

"The things *you've* done," Cayce said.

I wasn't sure how to respond.

I couldn't tell her the truth.

"What you did back there," she said, "I've never seen anything like it. You talked to them, Alex, like it was nothing, and they listened. I knew you were powerful. Everyone knows you're powerful. But you dismissed a horde of wraiths without so much as blinking. That language you were speaking, what was it?"

"I'll tell you later," I lied. "Right now, we've got a murderer to deal with, a murderer who uses the dead as a weapon."

Cayce pulled her cell phone from her pocket. "I'll call the chief."

"Not yet," I said. "I want answers first."

That wasn't the whole truth, either, but I didn't want to tell her that the cops weren't going to understand what I had planned for the killer. Well, they might. The chief himself seemed the type who wouldn't mind a little frontier justice. Hearing stories about ghosts and specters, though, even if you believe them enough to bring in a "ghost killer", isn't the same as witnessing it firsthand. One's concept of righteous retribution tends to change when one is shitting oneself.

Either way, I don't think we're getting paid for this job.

I wasn't filled with a lust for vengeance. I didn't know the people who had been murdered by the wraiths. I barely recognized that they even existed. I know, I know. That's a dickish way of thinking. But you get used to it when dealing with me. No, I wasn't after revenge. But I also didn't want someone out their dealing with necromancy in such a callous and casual way.

Whoever had summoned the wraiths was going to die tonight.

No one gets out of an encounter with wraiths unscathed.

I approached the house and climbed the steps. They shifted and creaked beneath my feet. Cayce followed, not far behind.

I didn't bother knocking. Instead, I grabbed the doorknob. I turned it. The door opened. I stepped inside.

The room beyond was dimly lit by strings of old Christmas bulbs. The red and green and blue glow flickered and blinked, revealing a ghastly effigy.

A scarecrow stood before me, the dusty, ratty, rotting uniform of a Union solider draped across a wooden framework. A burlap sack had been filled with God knows what and bound into place where a head might be. A grimacing face had been drawn in bleeding black marker onto the burlap. The figure's stomach had been stuffed with bones. Not the old, gnawed bones of cattle, but fresh, bloody human bones—bones that had been recently torn free of muscle and sinew and flesh.

"It's a beacon," I said. "This is what has been calling the wraiths into town."

Cayce didn't answer.

I looked to the door and saw she had not followed me in.

"It's all right," I said. "There's no one else in here. Whoever made this is gone. And it has no power, not anymore."

For a moment, she did not respond. I couldn't see her from where I stood. I wondered if she'd run off at the sight of the scarecrow.

"Cayce?"

The front steps creaked, and she moved through the door, a shuddering and hesitant gait. She was pale in the glow of the holiday lights. Her eyes were big and wet. Her lips trembled.

Blood spattered the floor at her feet.

I took a step towards her. "Are you—"

Cayce pitched forward, collapsing at my feet. The back of her jacket was ripped and torn in several places, punctured by a crude blade, and blood soaked into the clothing.

She had been stabbed, over and over again.

A figure surged through the open door, leaping past Cayce, tackling me, staggering me backwards, slamming me into the scarecrow. The effigy shattered around me as I crashed to the floor in a pile of moldy clothing and bloody bones. My attacker crouched on top of me, brandishing a butcher knife. Blood dripped down the blade, running down his fingers.

"Your fault!" he screamed.

He was tall, thin and boney, but strong.

He didn't blink.

"Your fault!"

I knew him.

Abram, the guy from the diner, the man who had offered Cayce his help.

He drove the blade toward my face.

I grabbed his wrist, keeping the knife only inches from my eye. His arm shook as he pressed forward. His eyes were wild. His teeth flashed. Spittle dripped from his lips.

"Your fault!" he cried.

With one hand, I held the knife away. With the other, I reached up and clawed at his face. My fingers found purchase in his left eye. I hooked my fingers, dug into the grape-like consistency of his eyeball, felt it rupture.

Abram screamed and fell away from me.

The knife fell from his fingers and spun across the floor as he feebly clutched at his face.

I scrabbled to my feet.

Cayce lay nearby, still, lifeless.

I prepared to say the words.

"Y-your damn fault!" Abram said. "You're the one they want!"

He hunched over and blubbered.

"Where did you learn how to speak to the dead?" I asked.

"They taught me the words!" Abram wept. "They said if I brought you here—"

The hairs on the back of my neck stood on end.

"You stole something." Spittle bubbled on Abram's lips. "You stole something and they want it back. They promised me. If I helped them—if I lured you out into the open—they'd bring my Martha-May back. They said they'd bring my sister back to me."

"Who—?"

But I already knew the answer.

My hand fell to the phylactery in my pocket. It was warm to the touch. Something within the vessel trembled.

The spirit within the glass was afraid.

Damn.

They had found me.

There's a reason I don't like helping people. Well, a few reasons. First of all—yes—I'm an asshole, as Cayce was so quick to point out. There's more to it, though. I have secrets only a few living souls know—and that knowledge comes with a certain amount of loathing and uneasiness and terror.

To understand what I am is to understand the frailty of life, death, and the afterlife.

The walls shuddered.

The floor bucked.

The ceiling heaved.

Abram curled his body into a fetal position. A cascade of twinkling lights—red, blue, green—flickered over him. He reached out with bloody fingers, grabbing blindly for the knife.

I didn't move to stop him.

I had more important fuckery to contend with.

Reality rippled around me. The room before me—Cayce's dying form, the shattered effigy, the Christmas lights, the murderous would-be necromancer—peeled away, and I could feel the other realm pulling at me like an undertow, trying to draw me in. I resisted.

Three figures stepped into view.

They were wreathed in painful light.

I held a hand up to shield my eyes.

These were the "beings of light" Cayce had encountered. They had visited her when she first arrived, examined her, determined she was not the prey they sought, and then let her go on her way.

The glow faded, and I saw them clearly. They were tall, strong and gorgeous, perfect examples of women, only they each stood nearly nine feet tall, the spires of their conical helms nearly brushing the ceiling. They had blue eyes and long blonde hair woven into braids. They wore gleaming armored breastplates and flowing white gowns. They held shields and spears.

The Valkyrie had come for me.

"Hello, ladies," I said.

Speaking with one unified voice they returned the greeting, only they spoke my true name, the name no living creature could know.

I hated the sound of it.

The room around me was returning to normal, the fracture between the realm of the living and the dead healing.

"If you wanted to see me," I said wryly, "you could have just asked nicely."

"You have hidden yourself," they said. They didn't so much speak as sing, their voices rising in unison, a painful dirge. The sound scraped at the roots of my teeth. "You have shrouded yourself in life so that you might remain unseen."

"Oh, that," I said. "Yeah. Fuck you."

"You betrayed us. You have taken that which does not belong to you. You cannot escape punishment forever."

"You haven't seen what I've seen. If you had—if you'd looked into those eyes—you would have done the same."

"Give the soul to us," they said.

In my pocket, the phylactery juddered in fear.

"I won't," I said. "It wasn't meant to die."

"You only prolong the inevitable."

"You can't understand what will happen. If you take it—if it dies—"

But I stopped.

The three shieldmaidens watched me coldly.

"You do understand," I said. "You know the consequences of what you're doing. You just don't care."

My anger swelled.

Again, I drew a breath, prepared to speak in the language of the dead. I had intended to use those words for Abram, but—

"They'll bring her back once you're dead!"

Abram leaped at me. He had the knife in hand once more and, as he slammed against me, I felt the blade punch through my stomach. He sneered and spat in my face. He twisted the blade, pulled it across my belly, and I felt my insides bulging out of the wound as I fell back with him on top of me.

"They'll trade your life for hers!" Abram said.

"They..." I could barely speak, "...lied."

The Valkyrie glided forward, not touching the dirty, gore-mired floor, pointing their spears toward me.

And—though it seemed an impossible task—I spoke at last.

"Take them."

The wraiths materialized like a sudden storm. Their tattered and torn bodies tumbled and rolled over one another. The gnashing bones that filled their bodies clattered and clacked and sluiced rancid blood.

"Take them all."

The Valkyrie recoiled as the wraiths swarmed at them, grabbing at them, tearing at their spears, pulling at their shields. The undead soldiers grabbed at Abram, too, yanking him to his feet, their fingers ripping into his stomach, tearing his guts out, leaving them in a pile on the floor as they stuffed him full of cattle bones.

All the while, Abram screamed.

He cried out in the language the Valkyrie had taught him.

"Please! Please, no! Please don't!"

But Abram's benefactors had not taught him an important lesson.

The dead don't recognize any value in "please."

The Valkyrie lashed out with their spears, but not even they could harm the dead, not while the dead obeyed my commands.

"Get them out of here," I gasped.

The wraiths howled with anger, condemning the Valkyrie, cursing them. The wraiths whirled through the air like smoke caught in a tornado, and they bore the Valkyrie and Abram with them, spinning in the air, tossing them around, whipping them to and fro. A pinhole of darkness opened at the center of the raging vortex. The wraiths dragged their prey toward the shadow, toward nothingness.

As quickly as they had arrived, they were gone.

I lay on the floor, panting for breath. My body was going cold. My blood spread out around me, mixing with Cayce's.

"Cayce," I muttered.

Painfully, I threw myself over onto my stomach and dragged myself toward her. She raised her head—slowly, weakly—to look at me. I think she might have died minutes earlier if not for the question that consumed her thoughts.

"Who are you?" she asked.

"You know who I am."

"I don't. Y-you're not just some necromancer. You said you'd tell me. Who are you?"

"I don't know how to answer that, not in the time either one of us has left. I've had many names. Many faces. I'm not sure that I know who I am myself."

"You're not human."

"I haven't always been." I pulled my hand away from my stomach. Blood poured from the wound. "Now, though, I'm all too human. If I wasn't, something so small as a knife to the gut couldn't possibly kill me."

Once upon a time...

And isn't that how fairy tales start?

But this was the end, not the beginning.

...I had been one of the host of psychopomps, one of the guides who takes fallen souls to the afterlife. I had been brother to the Valkyrie, to Charon, to Hermès, to the whippoorwills, to the dolphins. I had been counted as the greatest—

"We're dying," Cayce said.

"That's right."

No one gets out of an encounter with wraiths unscathed.

"I'm sorry," Cayce said. "I'm sorry I brought you into this."

"Me too."

She chuckled—or tried to. She coughed out a short, quick laugh, then winced in pain.

But it wasn't her fault.

Not really.

I had set these events into motion myself.

When I had fallen like a shadow upon a dying soul.

A soul that was not meant to die.

A soul that I could not allow to pass into the afterlife.

When I had turned my back on my brethren and been declared their enemy because of it.

I took the phylactery from my pocket. The tiny flask almost slipped from my fingers. It glowed, pulsing with light.

And I felt no pain.

Cayce, too, relaxed a little, her agony easing.

I had done the right thing. I knew it. The soul within the phylactery was not meant to die. It had been betrayed and with it all of humanity. Perhaps the cruelest trick of fate, though, was that I had somehow fallen into the role of its protector.

If I died, all would be lost.

The Valkyrie—or one of the other psychopomps—would come back and take the phylactery from my fingers. They'd open it. And when the soul poured out...

...they'd kill it.

I couldn't allow that to happen.

"Cayce," I said. "It's my turn to apologize."

"Why?" Her eyelids had grown heavy, her word slurred. "You didn't—"

I touched her face.

"No," I said. "I'm sorry for what I'm about to do."

I drew her soul from her body. I raised my hand, and cold vapor rose from her mouth, her nose, her eyes. She spasmed, arching her back, her body revolting at the idea of her soul being harvested. She grabbed at me, clawing at me with weak fingers.

Flesh likes to hold onto the spirit for as long as it can.

"Alex—" she pleaded. "Wait."

"I can't. If I wait, your soul will slip from your body. Another psychopomp will arrive to take you. And once they have you, they'll interrogate you. They'll torture your spirit to find out what you know about me."

"But I don't know anything."

"It won't matter to them. And you can't imagine how awful they can be. How cruel. You can't imagine how much pain you can feel, even after you're dead."

"Don't do this."

"I don't have a choice. If they harvest your soul, they'll know who you were. They'll know who I am. It will make hiding from them all the more difficult."

"But... what about what lies beyond? I wanted t-to see it. There's an afterlife."

"Not for you."

"Please," she whimpered.

But the dead—and the dying—don't place any value on the word.

"Rest," I said.

I cursed myself as I drew the last of her soul from her body. She flopped to the floor, spent and empty and cold. Her eyes stared at me in horror, but they saw nothing.

I used her soul like thread to stitch my wounds together.

***

Using another's soul to heal my wounds had changed me.

As I pulled away from the city of Centralia, I looked at myself in the Tahoe's side mirror. My eyes looked unfamiliar. The shape of my nose and mouth were different. The face I had worn before and the face of the woman I had damned to nothingness had become one.

My body had changed as well. I was a good ten pounds lighter, leaner, maybe an inch shorter. My fingers looked slimmer, longer.

And the changes went beyond the physical.

My soul had been reformed into one that had not existed until the night before.

If the psychopomps wanted to find me, they'd have to start their search anew.

This wasn't the first time I had changed my appearance. This wasn't the first time I had taken another's dying soul to heal myself.

I pulled up to a stop sign and let the car idle for a moment. I pulled the phylactery from my pocket. It was cool to the touch. It did not glow.

I hoped I was right.

I hoped it was worth all the terrible things I had done.

A black wagon rumbled along the road in front of me. An Amish wagon. I recognized the man at the reins. I recognized the boy who sat beside him. Isaiah. The boy stared back at me. He nodded.

I slipped the phylactery back into my pocket, took my foot off the brake, and got the hell out of there.

About the Creators

Cullen Bunn writes comic books, screenplays, novels, and short stories. He has written DEADPOOL, UNCANNY X-MEN, MAGNETO, FEARLESS DEFENDERS, and ASGARDIANS OF THE GALAXY for Marvel Comics. For DC, he has written SINESTRO and LOBO among other titles. His creator-owned comics include THE SIXTH GUN, HARROW COUNY, THE EMPTY MAN, METRO, BONE PARISH, and many others. He lives in Missouri with his wife and son. He once performed on stage as the World's Youngest Hypnotist.

Heath Amodio launched Hustle and Heart Films with founding partner Cullen Bunn in early 2018. He's an executive producer on their first three sold television series, and is developing another dozen projects with various production partners. He's the writer or co-writer on four upcoming 2020-21 graphic novels, and co-writer on an upcoming 2021 comic book series with his partner Cullen. (None have been announced yet.) He lives in Upstate New York with his Korean Jindo Bella.

Brian Quinn is one of the four Impractical Jokers. He was a firefighter with the FDNY in Ladder86. He co-hosts the podcast Tell Em' Steve-Dave on the Smodcast network. Along with Cullen Bunn and Walt Flanagan, he created the graphic novel Metro. He's also President of the world's first comic book themed motorcycle club, the Four Color Demons. In 2016 he became a Kentucky Colonel, just like Colonel Sanders, but without the chicken empire.

Brian Keene writes novels, comic books, stories, journalism, and other words for money. He is the author of over fifty books, mostly in the horror, crime, and fantasy genres. His 2003 novel, The Rising, is credited (along with Robert Kirkman's The Walking Dead comic and Danny Boyle's 28 Days Later film) with inspiring pop culture's recurrent interest in zombies. He oversees Maelstrom, a small press publishing imprint specializing in collectible limited editions, via Thunderstorm Books. He has written for such Marvel and DC properties as Thor, Doom Patrol, Justice League, Harley Quinn, Devil-Slayer, Superman, and Masters of the Universe, as well as his own critically acclaimed creator-owned comic series The Last Zombie. Keene has also written for media properties such as Doctor Who, The X-Files, Hellboy, and Aliens. The father of two sons, Keene lives in rural Pennsylvania with author Mary SanGiovanni.

Michael Patrick Hicks is the author of several horror books, including The Resurrectionists, Broken Shells, and Mass Hysteria. He co-hosts Staring Into The Abyss, a podcast focused on all things horror. His debut novel, Convergence, was an Amazon Breakthrough Novel Award Finalist in science fiction. He is a member of the Horror Writers Association.

In addition to writing his own works of original fiction, Michael is a prolific book reviewer and manages the High Fever Books website. His reviews have also been published by Audiobook Reviewer and Graphic Novel Reporter, and he has previously worked as a freelance journalist and news photographer in Metro Detroit.

Michael lives in Michigan with his wife and two children. In between compulsively buying books and adding titles that he does not have time for to his Netflix queue, he is hard at work on his next story.

Adam Cesare is a New Yorker who lives in Philadelphia. His books include Clown in a Cornfield, Video Night, and Zero Lives Remaining. He's an avid fan of horror cinema and runs Project: Black T-Shirt, a YouTube channel where he takes horror films and pairs them with reading suggestions. Clive Barker once called him "An author who knows how to make us afraid" and Cesare's never going to stop using that quote.

Kealan Patrick Burke, hailed by Booklist as "one of the most clever and original talents in contemporary horror," was born and raised in Ireland and emigrated to the U.S. a few weeks before 9/11. He has written five novels, among them the popular southern gothic slasher KIN, and over two-hundred short stories and novellas, including SOUR CANDY and THE HOUSE ON ABIGAIL LANE, both of which have been optioned for film. He lives in an unhaunted house in Ohio with a Scooby Doo lookalike rescue named Red.

Hustle & Heart Films was established by Heath Amodio and Cullen Bunn in early 2018 as a way to give creators more involvement in the adaptations of their work. They sold their first two shows in September 2018, a third in November 2019, and are currently developing a dozen more. Writer Heath Corson joined the team in 2019. H&H have several comic books and graphic novels planned for 2021 through Hustle & Heart Comics and other independent publishers.